VIBRANT

Heart

Corrissa James

ISBN: 0692338926

ISBN-13: 978-0692338926

Inkwell International

Laurel, NE 68745

www.inkwellinternational.com

VIBRANT

Heart

Chapter One

Melanie Olson swore under her breath and pulled the rented Ford Fusion onto the shoulder of the barely paved country road. She was already running late thanks to a delayed flight. Now a flat tire?

She got out of the car, her high heels sinking into the soft Nebraska dirt along the shoulder, and found the culprit: the rear passenger-side wheel. Looking at it more closely, she saw a nail as thick as her thumb stuck in the tire.

"Just great," she muttered. Glancing around, she noted the storm clouds moving in quickly from the west. The road, however, was deserted. "Naturally." She opened the trunk to dig out the spare. "All dressed up and actually in a position to use my feminine wiles for once in my life and not a single taker. Typical!"

She was only a few miles from her parents' house—no, check that, her father's house. She thought about calling for some help but tossed that idea aside. It was already time for the ceremony to start, and she couldn't interrupt the nuptials just because she wasn't dressed to change a tire. Knowing her luck, her dad would send Raymond out to help her. Her frown deepened. Being stranded and helpless was not the impression she planned for him.

She pulled out her weekend bag and set it on the ground next to the car, followed by her laptop and the wedding gift: a large crystal punchbowl. She smiled as she pulled back the flooring of the truck to reveal the spare tire and jack kit. The punchbowl was certainly beautiful, but its significance wouldn't be lost on her father. A shattered punchbowl had been the final straw, causing her mother to leave him.

Melanie focused on loosening the lug nuts. She was not a tiny girl by any stretch of the imagination. She looked most men in the eye and had enough meat on her that they didn't mistake her for some starving waif. But she wasn't a body builder, and she was beginning to think whoever attached the tire was. No matter how much she strained, the lug nut wouldn't budge. She redoubled her efforts, anxious to get the tire changed before the storm broke. She wouldn't have even bothered to come back for her father's wedding except she knew Raymond would be there, and she wanted to flaunt her new position as executive editor at GPP Press. Getting her hair cut and highlighted as well as finding the pale lavender dress that accentuated her curves in all the right ways would make it all the easier to remind him of what he had given up—and she couldn't wait to rub his nose in it.

The lug nut still wouldn't budge. This would not do at all. Calling her dad for help because she had a flat tire would be humiliating enough. Telling him she wasn't strong enough to remove the flat? Icing on the cake. Dammit! She was not going to let this stupid tire ruin her plans. She grabbed the bar and pressed against it with all her weight. The lug nut finally gave way, releasing against the pressure and sending her sprawling to the ground.

Her knees and palms were scraped and raw, her pale dress streaked with dirt, but Melanie didn't care. She had gotten the first lug nut loosened. It would all be downhill from here.

Then she felt the first raindrops, fat drops that plopped heavily into the dirt around her. Everything was still sitting out next to the rental car, and she scrambled to get her laptop and luggage stuffed into the backseat.

By the time she returned to fixing the tire, the rain was coming down so hard that her dress was plastered to her body and her dark hair clung to her face and neck. She tried to loosen the second lug nut, but her wet hands couldn't get any traction. The nut wouldn't budge.

"Are you freaking kidding me?" she screamed. So much for showing off to Raymond. She probably looked like a drowned rat. If she even made it to the ceremony in time—which was looking doubtful at this point—and Raymond was still there, he'd be heaving a sigh of relief instead of kicking himself for letting her get away. Of course, she probably wasn't going to see him anyway because she was stuck on the side of the road in an early afternoon thunderstorm.

"This is why I hate coming back here!" she yelled over the rain. "This. Right here!"

"Hey, darlin', you need some help?"

Melanie spun around to find a man standing in front of a classic Chevy pickup parked several yards back, its dim lights shining on her trunk. The man's broad shoulders—the kind that said he wasn't afraid of hard work—were hunched up under his cowboy hat. His denim shirt was wet enough that Mel could see the muscles working under it, and she had to admit, she definitely approved. But it was when she looked up into his face that her heartbeat went all erratic. His rich green eyes seemed to sparkle, even though the sun was hidden behind thick rain clouds, and the corners of his mouth curled up slightly in a perpetual smile. She fought the urge to run her hand along his jawline and trace the outline of his bottom lip with her thumb.

"Help?" Melanie cleared her throat. She chastised herself for getting all woozy over this cowboy, which was clearly not on the schedule. Suddenly furious that help hadn't shown up ten minutes earlier, she snapped, "No, I actually like standing here in the rain, *darlin'*."

The man pushed by her to the spare tire, turning his face away slightly, but Melanie still saw him laughing.

"Why don't you go sit in my truck where it's dry…darlin'." Melanie could tell he added the "darlin'" as an afterthought.

He loosened the nuts holding the spare as if they melted under his touch, and Melanie wanted to throw the nuts on the ground and stomp on the small, traitorous chunks of metal that were so pliable under his touch. Of course, who could blame them?

"How do I know you aren't some psycho who goes around stealing women from the side of the road?" Melanie snapped at him as he hefted the spare out of the trunk, the denim shirt pulling tightly against his arms and shoulders. He set the spare on the bumper, then turned to Melanie and smiled. Melanie leaned against the car for support as she drank in his strong jawline and emerald eyes. She half wished that he would steal her, take her into his truck, and let her press her body against his.

"Psychos don't actually change the tires before stealing the women, now do they, darlin'?"

And just like that, the spell was broken. He jacked up the car while Melanie gritted her teeth.

"Please don't call me that."

He moved to the far side of the car while Melanie stood by the trunk, waiting. She wished she could sit in her own car while he was changing the tire and dry off a little bit. She certainly wasn't going to sit in his truck. Luckily the rain started letting up. Although it didn't stop, it was certainly more tolerable.

"Now I never did get why women don't like being called that." He stood up to put the flat into the trunk.

Melanie just looked at him.

"'Darlin', I mean." He closed the trunk and leaned against the back of the car.

Melanie snorted. "Because it's belittling. And patronizing. And sexist," she said, crossing her arms. "Not that I expect you to understand that."

He took a step to walk past her, stopping just as they were shoulder to shoulder. "But a beautiful woman stranded in the rain on the side of the road? That's just damn sexy."

His husky laugh gave her goose bumps.

"I said sexist, not sexy!"

He was already climbing into his truck, watching her and laughing.

Melanie scampered into her car. She scowled into the rearview mirror, waiting for him to take off, but he just sat in his truck, waiting, which infuriated her even more. She rolled down her window and waved for him to go on by her. He didn't move.

"Fine, jerk," she mumbled under her breath as she rolled up the window. She put the car into gear and pulled onto the road, trying to ignore the hint of disappointment she felt because she wouldn't get to press her body against his after all.

Chapter Two

Jake Monroe hissed through his teeth when the woman tried to wave him on. The rental company's sticker on the back bumper confirmed his suspicions. She wasn't from around here, which was just fine with him because he was never going to get the image of her light purple dress clinging to her body out of his mind. He suspected that she'd planned such an effect, as the violet hues of the dress matched her violet eyes perfectly. And those damn eyes with their sparks of anger sent jolts through him that made it downright uncomfortable for him to be sitting here when what he wanted to do was kiss her anger away.

When she finally pulled out, he let go of the breath he'd been holding. It was a mistake. As he exhaled, he felt the desire surge through him. He pulled out onto the road and tried not to think about the driver of the car in front of him, but it did no good. All his thoughts led back to her. For a moment he debated flashing his brights at her, flagging her down and offering to take her for a drink until the storm clouds dissipated, letting her unwind and put her bad mood behind her. She'd order something sophisticated. A brandy perhaps. A few sips into it and she'd be relaxed enough to accept his offer of a shoulder massage—and even more if she were daring, and he suspected she was very daring.

"Dammit." He scowled. Thank God he would never see her again. She would be too dangerous to have around, too dangerous by far. His mother was right, though. He did need a woman. Maybe not in the same sense that his mother argued, but a man had needs and his needs were quickly approaching their breaking point.

Not that he hadn't had offers.

Working in small towns for a company with a strict no fraternization policy was perfectly fine for him—most of the time, anyway. But the places he worked seemed to all have one thing in common: their love for drama. He wanted no part of that. Drama was one of the reasons he'd left small towns in the first place. If he didn't love his job so much, he would never have returned to one—although Bender had been quite the welcoming town. And mostly drama-free so far. Only a few more months before his escape. He vowed to double down on the work and shorten that to a few weeks.

When she turned west, Jake swore loudly. She could not seriously be heading to the wedding? Of course she was—the rental car and the bags he'd noticed in the backseat, he should have figured it out. He followed her onto the same road, grimacing when her car sped up to put some distance between them. Definitely not from around here or she'd know that such a little car was likely to lose traction on the wet country road. Imagining her sliding into the ditch and needing to be rescued put a dangerous smile on his lips. Shaken up by such an accident, she'd be putty in his hands.

"Good Lord, Jake, what are you thinking!"

His mother was already going to ring his neck for being so late. If he had to call and say he'd been delayed by a good old-fashioned romp in the hay…well, his mom loved him, but possibly not that much. He slowed the truck. If the woman with the violet eyes wanted distance, he'd give her all the distance she needed. He could take a hint.

His cell phone buzzed. "Yeah, yeah."

He knew who it was without answering it. It only rang twice. His mother's signal. She hated cell phones, hated that people used them, and hated that Jake practically lived on his. She'd made him promise to turn it off before he arrived. The call was her final warning. It was too bad, really, because he would've liked to ask who the late-arriving guest was. The harder he tried not to think about her clinging dress and those electric eyes, the more prominent the vision became. Defiant, just like he imagined she would be. She wouldn't be putty for anyone; she'd be demanding in her passion, giving just as much as she got.

Jake groaned. He would never be able to control his arousal around her if he didn't get such thoughts out of his head.

Then again, why should he? Perhaps this was the perfect opportunity he'd been looking for. She was from out of town and didn't have enough luggage to be staying long. If he played his cards right, he could have the pleasure of that passion, taking care of his own needs in the process, without ever having to see her again.

He turned into the lane leading to the farm and parked his truck near several other cars, lined up along the lane. He practically jogged up the lane to make sure he caught up with her, his plan for seducing her falling neatly into place in his mind.

Chapter Three

Melanie glanced in her rearview mirror. Was he following her? Maybe he wanted something more from her. She remembered the subtle curl of his lips. They would certainly deliver a powerful kiss. She shook her head, dispelling that vision. He was probably coming for the wedding, although she hadn't recognized him as someone her father knew. A friend of the bride, of course.

Melanie hadn't met the bride yet. She tried to remember what her father had told her about his wife-to-be, but truth be told, she hadn't been all that interested in hearing about her father's love life when her own was so...nonexistent. The bride wasn't originally from Nebraska, but she'd moved to Bender about a year ago. Melanie couldn't remember from where—Minneapolis maybe? It was some big city, but that was all Melanie remembered because she'd been shocked that someone chose to leave the city to move to Bender, Nebraska.

Melanie saw Raymond's beat-up old Ford truck, his "Ray's Repairs" logo emblazoned across the tailgate, and smiled. She wasn't really here for the wedding anyway. Maybe her luck was finally turning. She parked close to his truck, making it impossible for him to leave without asking her to move her car. Now she'd be sure to run into him.

She pulled down the visor to look at herself in the tiny mirror. Her reflection was downright horrifying. Mascara and eye shadow had pooled in murky rings below her eyes. She was afraid to look any further, assuming her entire ensemble was ruined.

She glanced at her watch. The ceremony was scheduled to start in the barn at any minute. She could sneak into the house, clean herself up, and probably make it to the ceremony before it ended. Grabbing her still-damp luggage from the backseat, she headed for the back door to the house.

"Need a hand, darlin'?"

She couldn't stop the frustrated groan that escaped her lips. She wanted to turn around and educate this cowboy about his crassness but ignored him—partially to avoid his chiseled features, but mostly to hide her raccoon eyes—and stormed to the back door instead. She threw open the screen door and stepped forward. While holding it open, she twisted the handle on the main door.

The cowboy reached out and held the screen door for her.

"Thanks," she mumbled, just as someone opened the door from inside, nearly pulling her off balance. The cowboy grabbed her elbow to steady her, but Melanie jerked away, startled by the shock and warmth the contact spread throughout her arm.

A short blond woman stood in the doorway, her hands on her hips and a frown on her lips. "You think you can sneak in like this on today of all days?" The older woman shook her head and stepped aside, waving Melanie through the doorway.

Melanie fumbled with her suitcase, trying to push through the door as fast as she could so that the cowboy wouldn't touch her again.

"Oh Lord," the woman said to Melanie. "Honey, you're a fright. Don't just stand there, Jake. Be a gentleman and help her out."

"No, really, it's okay." Melanie finally got both herself and her suitcase through the doorway and into the mud room just off the kitchen.

"Nonsense!" The older woman put her hand on Melanie's arm. "Make 'em work for it, hon. They'll appreciate it later." She winked, as if the two women were sharing a secret, then turned to Jake. "Now you get her settled in upstairs, then you and I are gonna be having some conversating, young man."

"Yes, ma'am." Jake grabbed Melanie's suitcase and headed for the stairs at the far end of the kitchen.

"Don't you worry, darlin'," the woman said to Melanie. "You just get yourself cleaned up."

At the top of the stairs, Jake stood waiting for her. She didn't see her suitcase anywhere.

"I put it in the tub. Didn't want to get mud everywhere."

"Thank you." Melanie turned into the bathroom and slammed the door behind her.

Finally alone again, she leaned against the sink and sighed heavily, forcing herself to relax. The flight, the drive, the flat tire, the cowboy Jake—she'd survived it all. Now to clean herself up, go find Raymond, and show him what a mistake he had made letting her go. From this point forward, this weekend would be nothing but sweet satisfaction.

She looked in the bathroom mirror and saw that the visor mirror had been kind. She would need a total redo—and in record time. She toweled her hair off, pulled it into a loose ponytail, then washed all the makeup and dirt from her face, hands, and knees. The only other dress she brought with her, a soft turquoise sun dress that fell just above her knees, was a little too informal for a wedding. Then again, they were getting married in a barn, so it would have to do.

Car doors slammed outside. Were people leaving already? Surely they would stay for the reception. But what if Raymond didn't? He wasn't the schmoozing type, especially since he quit drinking. Melanie put on just a hint of mascara and a nice plum lipstick to highlight her best features. She pulled the ponytail holder from her hair and let her auburn tresses fall around her shoulders. The rain water had left her hair soft and radiant. She stepped back to survey the result. Not too bad—pretty without looking like she was trying too hard. She smiled. Raymond wouldn't stand a chance.

Chapter Four

Jake frowned at the bathroom door, considering whether he should throw it open and teach her a lesson about manners. Beauty was no excuse for being rude, and slamming doors went beyond rude, especially after he had helped her change her tire. Maybe he should have just left her stranded on the road, getting soaked by the rain. He turned his back to the door and counted to ten, clenching and unclenching his fists. It took him until nine to be able to push the anger back down. Picturing her clinging wet dress helped, although his anger was replaced with a new kind of intensity. Damn. He didn't realize just how long he'd gone without the feel of a woman beneath him, and now just the thought of this one was turning him into a jumbled mess.

Usually Jake's charm and smile could land the woman of his choosing in his bed—and all too often a woman not of his choosing. When he was younger, he had followed in his father's footsteps and bedded anyone who spread her legs for him. His mother had put a stop to that soon enough. She taught him to respect women, which he interpreted as being upfront and honest that he was only looking for a few minutes of fun, not a lifetime of commitment. After seeing how his father's roaming affected his mother—and how genuinely happier she was when she finally left the womanizer—he also understood the need to have only one play toy at a time and to not draw from the same pool right away. In the bedroom, he treated his lovers well, cherishing their bodies with his hands and his tongue, making sure they walked away just as satiated as he did. Of course, that approach only brought more women to his bed, including some incredible beauties who were adamant about never leaving it. Learning which women to avoid had not been without its own drama. Yet none had ever affected him as quickly or intensely as the woman on the other side of the bathroom door.

She was probably embarrassed by how the afternoon storm had ruined her outfit. He turned around and pressed his hands against each side of the door frame, leaning forward until his face was just inches from the closed door. If he said something to her now, told her how beautiful she looked despite the makeup running down her face, she'd hear him. But he bit his tongue and sat down on the top stair instead. Women didn't always appreciate such compliments, especially when they were upset about something. He imagined her without all the heavy eyeliner and bright red lipstick. A more natural look would let her violet eyes shine through. He wondered what she would look like first thing in the morning, her face clean, her hair mussed just enough that he would feel compelled to push a stray lock from her eyes.

"Aw, hell." He whipped off his cowboy hat and gripped it tightly until the brim was crushed. Those were the kinds of visions that he could not dwell on or he'd never make it to the ceremony. Instead of trying to compliment her, he'd bust through the bathroom door and turn on all his charm. He knew there were several bedrooms to take advantage of up here, and with everyone else at the ceremony…

She threw open the door, startling Jake. They stared at each other a moment, before she finally spoke. "I don't need a babysitter."

Jake stood, his eyes traveling the length of her body. "Maybe not a babysitter, but certainly a bodyguard." He nodded in approval.

She rolled her eyes and pushed past him. He fought the urge to reach out and touch her flowing auburn locks, especially as what he really wanted to do was grab her shoulders and pull her into an electrifying kiss. Scowling, he shoved his hat on his head and followed her down the stairs to the kitchen, where she was immediately cornered by the friendly blond. Jake groaned. His mother, God love her, was too much of a busybody by far.

"Oh sweetie, you look so much better. I thought we were gonna have to hose you off at first." His mother laughed, winking at the woman as Jake entered the kitchen. "Now you take this tray." She handed a tray filled with fresh strawberries, bananas, and oranges as well as various cookies to Melanie. "They just love my chocolate fountain! Can't get enough of it. And Jakey, make yourself useful and bring some more sodas." She glanced at Melanie. "I'm so glad you decided to come today. Jake's just as bad—I can never get him to come visit anymore. He's always too busy working."

Violet eyes glanced back at him, a hint of bewilderment evident. And something else. Did he see amusement spark in those violet enticing eyes? He bristled.

She didn't strike him as the kind of woman who used her looks to her advantage. Quite the opposite, in fact. He was pretty sure that she didn't know the power she could wield over men. So why would she be amused by his mother's chattering? Jake hefted up several cases of soda, more determined than ever to find out just who this woman was.

Chapter Five

Melanie let the blond woman rattle on as they walked outside and around the house. She was too busy trying to focus on her goal at hand to contribute much to the conversation. Having the cowboy walking several paces behind them was more distracting than the woman's chatter. Melanie turned her head back and forth, trying to release some of the uncomfortable tension. She wished Jake would go back to the kitchen or perhaps run an errand. He didn't need to be nearby when she ran into Raymond.

They rounded a corner and saw the barn, her father's pride. He had designed and built it himself. It didn't actually hold any farm animals or machinery; rather, it was her father's refuge. The main floor had moving walls that could partition off as little or as much space as needed for whatever project he was tinkering on. The upstairs loft was where her father liked to do "book work," as he called it, which was anything that didn't involve grease. The loft's wall of windows looked out over his eighty acres of farmland. When Melanie still lived at home, she would often find him in the loft, working late into the night. Sometimes she thought he even slept there, especially after he moved in an old couch he found at a garage sale. That was when Melanie realized that her parents' marriage wasn't as idyllic as it appeared.

The sofa was also where she and Raymond had first been together after he started staying in the barn. Melanie blushed at the memory. It was not her proudest moment. Raymond had shown interest in her but never acted on it—not until he fell off the wagon and Melanie found him fumbling with the lock on the barn door. They hadn't even done much that night, just kissing that led to some sloppy fondling. But the next morning, Raymond ushered her out into the early morning light as quickly as he could and tried to avoid her for weeks, despite her protests that everything was fine. Just when she thought she was past the humiliation of his rejection, he started meeting with her in secret once again, and everything seemed to be working out as she'd hoped. Then she got the publishing job. Now her cheeks burned as she remembered his empty promises to eventually join her in the city. Luckily the blond woman was too busy chatting away, talking about recipes and secret ingredients, to notice Melanie's flushed face. Melanie refused to look back at Jake, convinced that he could somehow see into her innermost thoughts.

In the barn, Melanie scanned the people standing in small groups, engrossed in their own conversations. No Raymond. Shuffling after the blond woman, she placed the tray of food on a long serving table set up along one wall, then moved to stand under the open stairway to the loft before she got sucked into another one-sided conversation with the chatty woman. From here she could look for Raymond while pretending to watch the clusters of people—and without being cornered by any of the guests, mostly members of Bender's small community. They meant well, but she could only tolerate their questions for so long, and their conversations invariably hinged on one idea: When was she going to move back and get married? They couldn't fathom the idea that someone might not want to live the quiet, rural life. They didn't understand that she liked the vibrancy of the city just as much as she liked the relaxed rhythm of the country.

Many of the faces were new to her—probably friends of the bride, although they could just as likely be friends of her dad. Melanie's dad was active in

Alcoholics Anonymous and was always bringing home "strays," as her mother referred to them. In fact, he had been Raymond's sponsor, which made Raymond family in her dad's eyes. When Raymond needed to sever all ties to his drinking buddies, he'd moved out to the farm and started working for her dad. Melanie had been in her final semester of college, although she still lived with her parents and helped out on the farm. She'd been immediately enamored by the tall, dark Raymond, who was undoubtedly wild at heart. The secretive nature of their relationship had made it all the more exciting. But clearly she'd found it more exciting than he had.

She licked her lips and smoothed her dress over her hips. He'd regret that decision now. If she could only find him.

"You don't really strike me as the wallflower type, darlin'."

Melanie groaned. Glancing over her shoulder, she saw Jake leaning against the wall, watching her. He nodded, tipping an imaginary hat to her, and she wondered where he'd left his cowboy hat. "Don't you have something better to do?" She didn't hide her irritation. "Serve the guests or something? Isn't that what you're here for?"

He chuckled, and she turned back to the crowd, furious that the delicious sound caused a warm shiver down her spine. Yes, Jake was a handsome man, but the only reason she was having such a strong reaction to him was because she hadn't been on a date in nearly two years. If her reaction was that strong toward Jake, how would she react when she saw Raymond? She became absolutely giddy at the thought.

"You know, if you keep pretending to be so focused on everyone else, you might hurt my feelings." He moved to stand next to her, their shoulders brushing. Melanie ignored him and tried to dismiss the energy that surged up her arm when they touched. He leaned over slightly and whispered against her neck, his warm breath causing the tiny hairs on her nape to stand on end. "Or is this your way of playing hard to get?"

"I'm looking for someone, if you must know. Someone who will be very, very happy to see me."

"Not as happy as me." He ran his fingers lightly up her arm, barely touching it.

Melanie was furious at the goose bumps emerging in the wake of his touch. He chuckled in her ear, which infuriated her even more. At least that's what she told herself—that the heat in the pit of her stomach was anger.

The blond woman passed by them, handing Jake a stack of empty trays before moving on to the door, probably to get more food. "Ah, duty calls."

Jake winked at Melanie before following the woman. Melanie was surprised that the woman seemed to have only one helper. Usually caterers brought a small army to parties. She turned back to watch the party-goers, glad that Jake was no longer there to distract her.

The small clusters of people parted as a tall, silver-haired man moved through them, heading for the table of food. Melanie stepped out from her hiding spot under the stairs as the man turned toward her and smiled, showing a row of perfect teeth. "Mel! You made it!"

"Hi, Daddy." She stepped up to throw her arms around his neck and kiss him on the cheek. "Of course I made it for your wedding, although I'm afraid a flat tire made me miss the ceremony."

He laughed, a deep, hearty laugh. "You ain't missed nothing yet. The preacher's having a heck of a time with one of his prized cows and won't leave her side until the calf is delivered."

Melanie shook her head. How had she lasted more than two decades here without going crazy?

"So have you met Evelyn yet?" He leaned closer so only she could hear him. "She's a little spitfire. But what a woman!"

Melanie leaned back and crossed her arms. "So is Mom," she said with a frown.

"Aw, honey, now I know your mama is a good woman, but she's happier down south."

Melanie nodded, knowing he was right. Her parents didn't resent each other after the divorce and had often said they just wanted the other to be happy. Her mother's life in Florida resembled nothing like life on the farm, but she didn't regret her country living. She often said it helped her grow into the person she was meant to be. So Melanie really couldn't play the guilt card on her father now.

"So where is she—Evelyn?"

"She's around her somewhere. Can you believe she insisted on making all the food herself?"

Melanie coughed several times, trying to clear the air trapped in her throat when she'd suddenly inhaled. The caterer was her father's bride?

"Oh, but here's someone you'll probably want to catch up with."

Melanie was still sputtering when she turned to see Raymond standing in front of her.

"Hey, Mel." His voice was as soft and calming as ever. He leaned in to hug her, and Melanie relaxed into the familiar smell of his aftershave. He had cut his nearly shoulder-length hair to a very short, neat haircut—the kind her father would find acceptable.

"Well, hi there." She tried to remember the lines she had rehearsed in the mirror for the last few weeks.

"Your dad tells me you're doing well in Chicago."

"I am. I really am." She flashed her most beautiful smile. He'd offered her the perfect opening, but she decided to milk it a bit before going in for the kill. "Look at you, looking all respectable and everything. Has the long lost boy finally grown up?"

Raymond nodded, looking almost like a little boy trying not to show how excited he was.

"Well, go ahead and tell her why," her father said.

Melanie glanced at her father, who was beaming with pride, then back to Raymond, who smiled bashfully.

He tugged on the elbow of someone talking in a neighboring group. "This is Anna." Raymond put his arm around a short, very pregnant red-headed woman. "The woman who changed my life."

Melanie reached out to steady herself as the room spun around her.

Chapter Six

Jake walked into the barn just as the woman with the violet eyes turned to greet Raymond Turner. Jake's jaw clenched, and he made a beeline for the small group. He'd had run-ins with Raymond before, although thus far both men had kept those encounters to themselves—Raymond out of self-preservation and Jake because his line of work required discretion. Warning signals were flashing in his mind to stay away from the small group of people surrounding the woman, but he pushed those warnings aside just in time to see the faint rosy flush in her cheeks turn to a sickly pale white. Something wasn't right, and he pushed through the guests to get to her side, grabbing her elbow just as he felt her arm go limp.

He stepped close, letting her lean into his warm body to steady herself.

"Here you are, darlin'."

He meant the term of endearment to be overheard by others, especially Raymond, whose stiffened reaction was almost amusing. Jake reaffirmed his message by brushing his lips against the woman's cheek. He felt her muscles tense in preparation for flight, but his solid grip on her arm held her steady. He glanced down at her and smiled softly, then winked. "Did you find your friends?" He glanced at the others around them, but made no move to let Melanie go. "She was so worried she'd miss everybody because of that flat tire."

"Well, lucky us that she got here in time," Raymond said, flashing first Jake, then Melanie an uncomfortable smile. "Sweetie, I don't think you've met Jake or Mel. This is my wife, Anna."

"Melanie, please," she corrected him, her voice tight. Melanie started to hold out a hand to the woman then faltered when Anna placed a hand on her swollen belly.

"Ugh, he's a kicker." Anna shifted on her feet, one hand rubbing her belly while the other was propped against the back of her hip.

"Looks like he'll be making an appearance any day now." Jake wanted to throttle Raymond, who hadn't taken his eyes off Melanie despite his wife's obvious discomfort. Instead, he pulled Melanie closer, grateful that she didn't push back against him and create a scene.

"We've got a few more weeks yet." Anna smiled, then glanced at the silver-haired man. "Just enough time for the wedding, Stan."

Stan threw his arm around Raymond's shoulder. "Wouldn't have been right without you two here. Jake, Raymond here is the one who helped me build the barn."

Jake nodded at the older man. "Oh, sure." He slid his arm around Melanie's waist. She didn't protest. For a moment, everything felt right.

His mother ended the brief interlude when she burst into their little circle, leading Reverend Jackson by the wrist. "He's here. Let's get this show on the road." Evelyn pushed through the group, grabbing Stan by the hand as she continued to the altar set up along the barn's far wall. Both the preacher and Stan let themselves be pulled along, which caused knowing laughter to ripple through the crowd.

As everyone turned to move closer to the couple, Melanie freed herself from Jake's grip. "Thank you," she mumbled, not looking him in the eye.

"Mmm hmm. I suppose I should be thanking Raymond?"

She jerked her head up to glare at him, fury erupting on her face.

Jake leaned closer to her, until his face was just inches from hers. "After all, your swooning over a married man meant I got to kiss you."

"Ha!" Melanie rolled her eyes. "As if that were a kiss."

Before she could walk away, Jake reached out and pulled her to him until their lips were pressed together. It was a gamble, and he knew it. She could very well pull away, causing quite the scene. But she didn't. Instead, her lips parted as her hands slid up his arms to his chest, leaving a trail of fiery desire. His tongue teased at her lips. When she pressed closer to him, he groaned and pulled back, ending a kiss that he wanted to spend the rest of the day exploring. He told himself to step away, that he was playing with fire with this woman, but he couldn't bring himself to remove his arms that still encircled her waist.

Stan cleared his throat loudly. Melanie turned to see the entire crowd staring at her and Jake. Her face burned red, and she hid it in Jake's chest, his arms coming up to hold her protectively. He chuckled at her embarrassment, trying to distract his body from the fact that he could smell the peach-scented shampoo from her hair and feel the curves of her body fitting so precisely into his. She tried to pull back, but his arms kept her firmly in place.

"Sorry, folks," he said to the guests. "Guess we got swept up by the romance of the day."

The guests laughed, and some applauded. As the couple turned back to the altar, Jake's hold on her eased. Melanie pulled herself away from him and stepped back, raising a hand to slap him. Stan's words stopped her in mid-swing.

"Son, you'll have to save it for your own wedding. For now, get my daughter up here so we can get this ceremony over before your mother hog ties us both."

Daughter? Understanding hit Jake like a fist to the gut, and suddenly he was wishing he had just left her by the side of the road. He had created a mess of it all now, and it would only be getting messier because he would be sharing another kiss with Melanie Olson. Of that he was certain.

Chapter Seven

Melanie reeled with the realization that Evelyn, her new step-mother, was Jake's mother. She had just made out with the bride's son at her father's wedding while all the guests watched. Including Raymond and his pregnant wife. She swallowed, trying to push down the embarrassment that she was sure was evident on her face.

Jake placed his hand just above her elbow to lead her to the altar, but she jerked her arm away, her face burning even brighter. She stormed up to the two steps to the dais, refusing to look at anyone as she moved to stand next to her father.

"Over here, sweetie," Evelyn said in a hushed voice, waving Melanie to her side.

Melanie glanced first at Evelyn, then Jake, who was standing just next to the dais, smirking at her.

How dare he laugh at her when this was all his doing. If he had just left her alone when she'd made her distaste known the first thousand times, she would not be standing up in front of more than a hundred people anxious for the ceremony to finish so they could call their friends with the latest gossip. She ground her teeth, threw back her head, and took her place next to the bride.

"All right, preacher," Evelyn said. "No more stalling. Let's make this official."

Melanie could barely keep her attention focused on the preacher's words. When the ceremony ended and the newlyweds were making the rounds with their guests once again, Melanie tried to make her way toward the door to sneak out unnoticed. Unfortunately, Evelyn had eagle eyes. Each time Melanie moved a bit closer to the exit, Evelyn was suddenly by her side, ushering her back into the crowd to meet a friend or cousin of hers, saying, "And this is my beautiful new daughter," followed by a wink and a smile. Melanie was mortified by what people must be thinking in light of her recent public display with Jake, but she didn't want to ruin Evelyn's fun. It was her wedding day after all. Besides, her father would read her the riot act if she offended his new bride.

The one good consequence of being ushered around by Evelyn was that she shooed Jake away every time he got too close to them, although usually by making a comment that made the guests laugh and Melanie's face burn in embarrassment. Jake seemed completely unfazed by his mother's reminders that he'd already welcomed Melanie to their family. He would move away, but never too far, so Melanie was constantly aware of his presence and his deep emerald eyes following her.

Soon Evelyn was introducing Melanie as a big city writer, patting the younger woman's hand with pride as she asked Melanie to share her latest projects. Melanie didn't have the heart to correct her and explain that she had abandoned writing to work full time as an acquisitions editor, but she was able to name drop a few of her bigger-named clients, which led to oohs and ahs and questions about what they were really like. Before Melanie realized it, she had forgotten all about her pre-wedding embarrassment and was enjoying herself. It helped that Evelyn's family and friends were certainly entertaining.

Melanie was introduced to a group of three little old ladies all dressed in varying shades of pastels, each with blue-tinted hair that matched their polyester dresses. "These are my aunts: Rose, Lily, and Daisy," Evelyn said. "Spinsters the lot of them." She winked at the women, who cackled in response.

"Oh, you are incorrigible, Evie," Lily said. "Spinsters my tiny wrinkled patootie."

"Spinsters who have married more men than you bothered to invite to this shindig," Daisy said.

"Married and buried," Rose corrected.

Daisy shushed her sister, then turned back to Evelyn. "Where are all the single men you promised, anyway?"

"I never promised you anything, auntie." Evelyn laughed and rolled her eyes at Melanie.

"Bull puckey," Lily said. "I heard it myself. You told us to come and enjoy the meat market."

Melanie bit her lip to keep from laughing too hard.

"What about Jake?" Rose said.

"What about him?" Evelyn said.

"Maybe he's got some single friends and can hook an auntie up," Rose said.

Lily waved Jake over to join them. He kissed each aunt on the cheek, and they in turn batted their eyes at him.

"So where are all the single men, Jake?" Lily asked. "We're looking for the real action."

Jake affected a sheepish expression as he smiled at his great-aunts. "I invited some friends, but they were all afraid they wouldn't be man enough for you."

Rose and Daisy laughed, but Lily harrumphed loudly.

"You're no help," Lily said. "Especially now that you're all googly-eyed over this one." She pointed at Melanie, who tried to laugh and brush the comment off.

"Be nice, Lily," Daisy said. "Don't embarrass the young lovers."

"Oh, we're not—"

Before Melanie could finish, her father interrupted them to inform Evelyn that they were running low on ice.

"Shoot, I was afraid of that. The rainy day meant even the farmers showed up today, and they are a celebratory bunch." She looked at Melanie and shrugged, then turned to Jake. "Sweetie, will you make a run into town for more supplies? Oh, and Melanie, can you go with and get some more drinks? Last time I asked Jake to get sodas, he came back with four cases of generic cream soda." She stuck her tongue out in disgust.

Melanie opened her mouth to argue, then thought better of it. Driving into town would give her the perfect opportunity to talk to Jake. She didn't want him to think that he could go around kissing her whenever he felt like it. And if he was driving, he wouldn't be able to sneak up on her again and do something unexpected, no matter how good it felt.

Chapter Eight

The walk to his truck was cloaked in a strained silence punctuated by their footsteps in the gravel. Finally Jake couldn't stand it anymore.

"So, what do you think of these crazy kids getting married?" He flashed Melanie a goofy smile, hoping that his attempt at humor wasn't failing as badly as he thought it was.

To his surprise, she smiled back. "Kids these days, right? You try and tell them not to rush into anything, they've got their whole lives ahead of them, but do they listen? Of course not."

They glanced at each other before laughing. Jake hurried the last few steps to open the door for Melanie, bowing low in mock servitude as she slid into the truck.

"You're not leaving, are you, Mel?"

Jake scowled at Raymond, who was hurrying down the lane after them.

Melanie shook her head. "Ice run. Don't worry, I'll be back soon."

Jake slammed the door, gave Raymond a withering glare, and headed for the driver's side. Sliding in behind the wheel, he said, "He's married." He started the truck. "And soon to be a father."

Melanie didn't look at him, instead rolling down the window and waving at Raymond as they drove away.

They traveled down the country roads for several miles in tense silence, passing fields full of corn and soybeans. The earlier storm had moved on, leaving behind vibrant green corn stalks contrasted with the grayish-green of the soybeans and the yellow-greens of the mighty cottonwoods crowding around invisible creeks. The smell of the rich dirt in the fields wove through the truck. Melanie stuck her arm out the window, letting the wind caress her hand as they drove.

Jake interrupted the silence. "You can do better than Raymond Turner."

Melanie rolled her eyes, her light-hearted laugh sounding more like choking. "You don't know anything about him, the demons he's overcome."

Raymond's demons were public knowledge, especially at the local hotel bar, where everyone could watch his escapades with the women who passed through town. Unfortunately, not enough women stayed overnight in Bender on a regular basis, which left Raymond to hit on the wait staff. Jake frowned, completely at a loss as to why Melanie would tolerate Raymond's antics. She clearly wasn't afraid to give someone a piece of her mind, and he'd seen how she'd reacted when introduced to Raymond's wife. Was Melanie one of Raymond's extramarital pastimes? The idea didn't sit well with him. He just couldn't picture Melanie agreeing to be the other woman for anyone. He recalled their kiss, how passionate she'd been. Had that all been a show for Raymond?

Jake shook his head. He didn't like where his thoughts were taking him. He didn't know what kind of relationship she had with Raymond and didn't care. He was just looking for a good time. If that good time happened to be with one of Raymond's playthings, well, that could be an added bonus. He didn't think Raymond would be all that appreciative of someone, especially Jake, showing one of his women a better time. The thought caused a satisfied grin that Jake couldn't hide.

As they pulled into town, he slowed the truck but continued past the store.

"Aren't we going to stop?"

He shrugged, but said nothing else. She went back to looking out the window.

She pointed to the new building on the corner of the town's main street. "Is that the new hotel?"

"Yup."

"Nicer than I expected."

"What's the matter? You think everything in a small town has to be run down?"

"No, of course not." Melanie frowned. "It's just, it's changed since I left. This hotel wasn't here before, so when I made reservations, well, honestly, I expected a drive-up motel. That would be more befitting of a town with only a few thousand people. That place looks…"

"Modern?"

She nodded. "Modern and inviting. Almost like an upscale spa."

Jake glanced at her. "It's amazing what a little investment can do for a small town."

"I guess so."

"Plus the taxes the city gets from the hotel have enabled them to update the old, pothole-filled road here with a wider two-lane road, complete with stately street lamps reminiscent of a bygone era."

"I'm surprised they get much business, though. Bender isn't exactly a center of tourism."

Jake nodded. It was a comment he'd heard hundreds of time. "Yes, but tourists aren't the only people who use hotels. Bender's at the crossroads for two major highways, and the nearest hotels along either of those highways are an hour away. For anyone driving through—"

"It's like an oasis!" She chuckled. "Smart investors."

He noted the ease in her voice as she took in the familiar sights. She swiveled around, looking for the places she knew. Her curiosity was mesmerizing for him. She touched his arm to draw attention to her childhood friend's home and the corner where she helped plant daisies as a city beautification project. She clapped in excitement at the tall white flowers welcoming her home. He nodded to each of her comments, but he couldn't take his eyes from her excited expression. The intensity of her anger had driven him mad with desire, but the sincerity in her animated movements now stirred something much deeper than his passion, something he had never experienced before.

He headed toward the business district—all two blocks of it—and pulled up alongside the curb at the end of the street. He turned off the truck, pointing to a large brick building with giant tinted windows. "The hotel investors also contributed to the new library."

"Seriously?"

"You like it?" The building looked like it had stepped out of the pages of a fancy architecture magazine.

"It's beautiful. When I lived here, the library was a tiny one-room building that was barely bigger than my bedroom."

Jake put his arm along the back of the seat and ducked his head to look out the passenger-side window, wishing she hadn't mentioned her bedroom. "Yeah, the owners of the new hotel offered some matching funds, and the townspeople really rose to the challenge. It was just supposed to be updates to the old building—a new roof, an air-conditioning system, some new computers—but they raised the money for this."

"I just can't imagine." Melanie's voice trailed off for a moment. "Is it open? Can we go inside?"

He chuckled at her excitement. "Sorry. Not many people visit it on Saturday afternoons."

"No, of course not. Although they always had to kick me out at closing time." She giggled and leaned back against the window. "I used to drive my parents crazy just so they would want me out of the house. On more than one occasion my mom was all too happy to drive me into town and drop me off."

"You led quite the rebellious life. Although that explains why you got the writing bug."

Melanie shrugged. "I suppose."

"Strange."

Melanie raised an eyebrow in a silent question.

Jake smiled. "Most authors are all too eager to point to reading as the spark that set them on their lifelong path."

"For me it was more about escapism." She leaned against the door, closing her eyes as the sun washed over her face. "Reading told me what the big wide world out there was like, and all I wanted was to be out in it, away from here. But of course, if I hadn't been so quick to run to the library all the time, I might have seen how much trouble my parents were in."

"Was it all you thought it would be?"

She opened her eyes halfway and looked at Jake, who was now looking out the driver's side window. "What do you mean?"

"The big wide world."

"Oh." She gave him a half smile and a shrug. "There is so much I love about the city—the energy and vitality of all those people coming together in one huge mass of intensity—just like I love the freedom of driving down country roads in the summer, the windows down and the wind running through my hair. But is anything ever as perfect as you expect it to be?"

He laughed. "No, not really." He smiled as Melanie relaxed again, letting her eyes close. "Then again, some things are better than I could have ever imagined." He slid across the seat to kiss her lightly on the lips. Before she could put up her hands to push him away, he returned to his place behind the wheel. "Wasn't my imagination. You do taste like raspberry." He started the truck and winked at her as he licked his lips.

Chapter Nine

They made the drive back to the house in silence, although for different reasons. Melanie was pretty sure that Jake was proud of himself for putting her back on edge. When he started humming as he drove, she became even more convinced of his gloating. Meanwhile, she was stewing at his ability to make her insides flutter with a quick peck on the lips.

She couldn't really be surprised that the unexpected attention from Jake was causing her body to react in such powerful ways. It had been so long since her last date. She'd been saving herself for Raymond, convinced that once he saw how she had succeeded in Chicago, he would beg to be part of her life again. He'd been so worried that life in the big city would change her that he'd refused to risk it. But she hadn't changed. She'd thrived—and waited patiently for the chance to step back into his life.

Yet now he had Anna and Melanie had no one.

She tried to remember when she'd last gone out with someone, but her thoughts were continually interrupted by the memory of Jake's kiss in the barn. It really had been a delicious kiss, and if they had met in Chicago, she'd have been thrilled to see where it went with him. But she would not go through this again, a long-distance relationship with someone from the country, not after Raymond. And she certainly wasn't going to move back and become a farm wife.

No, now she just needed to focus on surviving until she could return to Chicago, where she would go out with every guy she could until she found someone who could kiss just as well as—no, better than!—Jake. Maybe she'd sign up with one of those dating services. Finding someone in Chicago would allow her to make a complete and clean break with Nebraska.

As soon as Jake pulled the truck to a stop in front of her father's garage, Melanie had her door open and was heading into the house.

"Oh heavens, sweetie," Evelyn said when Melanie stepped into the kitchen. "You look as white as a sheet. Are you feeling okay?"

"I'm just a little tired." Melanie ignored Jake as he walked in behind her. "It's been a long day, and I think the traveling is catching up to me."

Evelyn grasped her hand and patted it. "Of course, of course, sweetie. You go on upstairs and lie down for a bit. The party will still be here when you feel up to it." She nudged Melanie toward the stairs.

Melanie didn't need much encouragement. Putting the sounds of Evelyn and Jake preparing more refreshments for the guests behind her, she went straight to her old room, which was now a guest room, although the furniture was the same as when she lived there. She removed her dress and draped it over the desk chair, then climbed between the sheets, deeply inhaling the crisp, fresh smell. The familiar feel of her old bed was relaxing, and she closed her eyes.

Jake's smiling face came to life behind her eyelids. Melanie groaned and rolled over, turning her back to the room's door, as if that would somehow block out the thoughts of him. Instead, he started laughing at her, like he somehow knew that he was tormenting her in her thoughts. It was a deep chuckle, the kind that Melanie knew made his chest rumble. She remembered how it felt to rest her cheek on his chest, his arms closing around her protectively. She could almost smell the mix of his earthy cologne and light sweat from the afternoon's humidity. She told herself to stop this line of thinking, that it wouldn't help her relax. Then again, she'd been trying to block these thoughts all afternoon and it hadn't done any good. Maybe letting her thoughts run wild would finally get it all out of her system and make it easier to at least be in the same room as Jake.

Jake had shown her that he could arouse her excitement in an instant, but he had also been playful at times. No doubt he would be intense in bed—passionate and skilled, yet his polite charm suggested he would be caring about his partner. If she had let the kiss continue, their tongues probing and twisting and dancing while their hands explored each other's bodies—his muscular arms and chest, his abdomen tightening reflexively as she swirled her fingers across it in gentle circles, his hands moving down her back, pressing her tighter to him, her breaking their kiss to lean back and expose her neck while she moaned his name....

"Oh, darlin'."

His voice, deep and husky, penetrated her ecstasy as if from a distance. He dotted her throat with love nibbles, leaving a hot path of arousal until he reached her earlobes.

"Oh, Mel."

His hot breath in her ear created molten lava deep inside her, and she turned toward him, moaning softly, begging for more, but unable to form the words. Luckily he didn't need words. His mouth was no longer tender, but voracious as it seared down her neck and across her shoulder.

Melanie frowned. His kisses were no longer passionate sparks aimed at exciting her senses. They felt wet, sloppy even. She tried to clear her thoughts, return them to the moments before, when her skin felt like it would start on fire, but the sticky wetness on her neck wouldn't go away.

"Oh, Mel."

Melanie's eyes flew open. She wasn't dreaming, there really was someone in the room with her. She jerked away, throwing herself onto the floor on the far side of the bed. How dare he come into her room, uninvited! The nerve of him—did he just think all women would drop their panties for him? "Just what do you think you're doing?" she shrieked, standing up to face the bed.

"Mel, honey, what's wrong?"

She blinked several times, trying to adjust to the shadowed room. Had she actually fallen asleep? The darkening windows indicated that the sun was setting outside.

"Sweetie, it's okay."

She took a step toward the bed. "Raymond?"

"Of course it's me." He laughed. "Come on back to bed." He patted the bed lightly. He wasn't wearing a shirt.

Melanie suddenly wanted a scalding hot shower. She hoped he hadn't removed any other articles of clothing. "What are you doing? You're married!"

"C'mon, Mel. Don't worry about that."

"Worry about it? Worry about it!" She couldn't stop herself from yelling. All the emotions of the day boiled up inside her, and her frustrations were aimed at the half-naked man lying in her bed. She moved around the bed, snatching up his shirt from the floor and throwing it at him. "Get your sorry ass out of my bed right now, mister—take your clothes and just get out!"

Raymond jumped up and grabbed Melanie in a tight embrace, pinning her arms down by her sides. "Oh, Mel, honey, it's okay." He drew out each syllable, creating a sickeningly sweet whine. "Don't tease me like this. You know it makes me crazy."

When she struggled against him, he tightened his grip. "Let me go," she hissed, but he only laughed. Frustrated, she did the only thing she could think of: She bit his shoulder. Hard.

Raymond squealed and jumped back. "Jesus, woman. What are you doing?"

"What I should have done a long time ago." She smiled in victory as he rubbed at his shoulder, checking for blood.

He grabbed his shirt from where it had fallen on the bed and hastily shrugged into it. "I don't know who you think you are, Miss Big Shot, but I don't play that way. I've got a wife, remember?" He nodded to Jake, who was standing in the doorway, his hand on the doorknob, his face contorted in black anger. "Be careful with this one." Raymond pushed by Jake. "She likes it rough."

Jake stared at Melanie, who felt the victory drain from her body. How much had he heard? Surely he didn't think that she wanted Raymond in her bed!

"My mother thought you might like to know that some of the guests are starting to leave." His voice was clipped and icy. He was barely keeping his anger in check. He turned to leave.

"Wait—"

He called back over his shoulder. "And put some damn clothes on!"

Melanie glanced down and realized that she was still in her underwear. She took two steps and slammed the door shut, her cheeks burning a bright red. She was never going to be able to live down this embarrassment.

Chapter Ten

Jake didn't bother saying goodbye to his mother or Stan. Or anyone else still at the reception, which would likely last well into the night. He wouldn't risk running into Raymond, knowing he would pummel the man—the snake—with his fists until he was begging for mercy. But if he stayed in the house, he would risk seeing Melanie, and he was even more terrified of what he would do to her. Instead, he stormed out to his truck and tore off down the country roads. He rolled down the windows and cranked up the radio, but nothing could block out the memory of what he'd seen: Melanie, half-naked, her angry eyes sparkling.

Sparkling in anger at Raymond, he reminded himself. A lover's quarrel.

He turned onto the highway, gagging on the bad taste it left in his mouth. Melanie didn't seem like the kind of girl to fall for a married man, especially one like Raymond. Jake didn't understand why any woman would fall for his charms, but they did. He'd seen it with his own eyes. Yes, usually the women were either clearly desperate themselves or feeling charitable for the evening. He couldn't envision Melanie as either of those.

He could only envision her in that damn lacy bra and panties. The bra and panties she had worn for Raymond.

When he pulled into the parking lot at work, he was practically growling. He went in the back door to avoid seeing anyone, although Saturday nights were usually pretty slow in the hotel's business offices. He sat at his desk and flipped on the computer, then spent the next half hour staring at the screen, trying to get Melanie out of his thoughts, chastising himself whenever he caught his mind wandering to her raspberry lips or her curves that fit so well into his. But it was when he imagined her eyes looking up into his that he nearly lost control. Reminding himself that she wanted to be looking up at Raymond instead only made him want to break something.

He considered calling Stan. He didn't think her father would be too happy about the hired help sleeping with his daughter, especially given Raymond's impending fatherhood. Jake ran his hands through his hair. He couldn't stand Raymond, but it was clear that Stan thought of him as a son. There was no way Jake was coming between that bond, especially if it meant making Stan choose between Raymond and Melanie. Stan would choose Melanie without a doubt, but Jake knew from his own father's philandering that once such secrets got out, they had a way of wreaking havoc on the relationships of everyone involved. He wouldn't do that to his mother and Stan, and he certainly wouldn't do that to Melanie.

He sat back in his chair, exhaling slowly. Why did he care so much about protecting Melanie? He tried to convince himself that he was concerned about the sanctity of his mother's new marriage, but he knew he was lying to himself. He glanced at his watch. He'd known Melanie for less than twelve hours, yet every moment without seeing her dragged on as he tortured himself with thoughts of who she was with and what she was doing with him. This was not healthy.

He headed to the front desk, glancing into the restaurant and bar as he passed. He nodded at a few of the regulars, then frowned at one regular in particular.

At the front desk, he signaled for the receptionist. He wanted to talk to her away from prying ears. Not that he expected anyone to be listening, but he insisted on discretion even when they weren't busy. "Is Trish Cassidy working tonight?"

The overnight receptionist, a college student who used the quiet hours to study for exams, rubbed her eyes. "Trish? No sir, Mr. Monroe. I checked the moment I saw Bruce walk in."

Jake nodded. He trained his staff to be discreet, but not stupid. Bruce Garrison was overly possessive of his girlfriend, Trish, who waited tables for the hotel. "I've got my cell on. If he even sneezes too loud, you call me first. You got it?"

"Yes, sir."

He turned to head back to his office, shaking his head. Small towns and their drama. He could never escape it, whether from his staff or now his family. On a whim, he stepped back to the front desk. "Has Melanie Olson checked in yet?"

The college student stifled a yawn then blushed. "Sorry, chemistry exam on Monday." She shrugged. "Did you say Olson?"

"Yeah, would've been in the last half hour or so."

"No one's checked in since I came on duty about two hours ago."

"Okay."

"You want me to let you know when Ms. Olson checks in?"

He shook his head. "No, that's okay. Actually—" He paused. "Yes, do let me know. And do me a favor. Put her in the king upgrade room."

"Yes, sir. Anything else?"

He smiled. "Yes. Ace that chem test."

Jake walked back to the bar and sat down at the end closest to the kitchen door. From here he had an unobstructed view of Bruce Garrison, who was nursing a beer. By the looks of his bloodshot eyes, it wasn't his first. Jake smiled to himself. It was only a matter of time before Bruce got himself in trouble, and Jake would be here to handle it. If he couldn't release his frustration with Melanie, he'd just have to release it the old-fashioned way.

Chapter Eleven

Melanie calmed herself down enough to get dressed, but by the time she made it out to the barn, her embarrassment had turned to fury. Jake had no right to be angry at her, to jump to the obvious conclusion that he did. But she was ready to give both him and Raymond a piece of her mind. Only about half of the guests remained in the barn, most of them paired off and dancing to 1960s music piped through a small stereo in the corner. Neither Jake nor Raymond was among those still enjoying the festivities. She found her father and told him she was heading to the hotel for the night.

"You sure, sweetie? There's plenty of room here, and Evelyn really wants to get to know you better." The dejection on her father's face was evident.

Melanie flashed her father a telling smile. "Oh, Daddy, it's your first night as man and wife. You should have the house to yourself." She winked at him and tried not to laugh when he blushed. "Besides, I feel a migraine coming on, so it's probably best that I go crash for a while. How about we all meet up for lunch tomorrow afternoon before I head back. Say around 12:30?"

"Better make it 1:00. The preacher has gotten long-winded in his old age, especially in his Sunday morning sermons." Her father rolled his eyes playfully. "We'll meet you at the hotel restaurant."

Melanie hugged her father quickly before Aunt Rose hauled him back onto the dance floor.

During the drive to town, Melanie tried to take stock of the weekend so far. Absolutely nothing had worked out the way she had planned. Raymond was not only married, but she was finally able to see him for who he really was. What bothered her most was that, deep down, she always knew he was less than ideal. He could be incredibly charming when he wanted something, but he hadn't wanted to share in her life, hadn't wanted to celebrate her successes. He hadn't wanted her.

Not until he thought that Jake wanted her.

Jake was something else she had not counted on. She knew that her father's new wife had a son, but that was the only information her father had ever shared. Not that Melanie had asked for any. Besides, what did she expect her father to tell her? Be prepared to meet Evelyn's son, who will make your insides melt and your toes curl when he kisses you? She laughed at the thought as she parked the rental car, then consoled herself that she wouldn't have to see Jake until maybe Christmas. Hopefully by then his presence wouldn't have such a strong effect on her. As soon as the thought crossed her mind, she knew it wouldn't be true, but she was determined to pretend otherwise, at least for the rest of the weekend.

Her room at the hotel was simple, clean, and full of hidden treasures, like the soft, thick towels in the bathroom, the overstuffed chair and ottoman tucked into the corner between the bathroom and the bed, and the basket of goodies left on the small table next to her second-floor balcony. The attached note indicated that the candies, cookies, apples, berries, and cheese were all products made in Nebraska and compliments of the hotel. It also indicated that a bottle of wine from the winery just down the road was included in the mini-fridge. It was all definitely a luxury not commonly offered in small towns. She grabbed an apple and ate it while undressing, realizing she hadn't eaten anything since the early breakfast before her flight. She glanced at the basket of food just before heading into the bathroom. "You're all mine when I come out." She laughed at herself, then jumped in the shower, letting the hot water soothe her muscles.

She managed to avoid thinking about Jake for all of one minute. As soon as he popped into her mind, she distracted herself by reading the labels on the little bottle of shampoo, lathering up her hair and rinsing it (twice!), combing conditioner through every single strand of hair, and then counting to 180 to make sure she left it on long enough, although she did have to start over several times when her brain decided that studying Jake's perfect smile was more interesting than simply counting. When her thoughts turned to imagining taking a shower with Jake, she turned off the water and briskly dried herself off. "No more of those kinds of thoughts—not now, not ever." She put on the robe she found hanging on the back of the door and ignored the little voice laughing in her head.

She found a corkscrew on top of the mini-fridge, popped open the wine—a nice Willow Blush that warmed her cheeks—then collapsed in the overstuffed chair, the basket of goodies in one hand and the remote control in the other. She flipped through the channels, looking for an action movie to watch. Nothing with a sappy love story line. Explosions and gunfire were what she needed. Finally settling on a martial arts movie dubbed into English, she poured the last of her wine into her glass just as a knock sounded on the door.

The bedside clock showed just after 11:00. Cinching the robe more tightly about her and wondering if the television was too loud, although she didn't think so given that she could barely hear it herself, she looked through the peephole and groaned.

"Open up." Jake spoke quietly, but firmly, staring directly into the peephole from the other side. "I'm not leaving 'til we talk."

Melanie sighed and opened the door, knowing he very likely would stand out in the hall all night if she made him. "It's late. Can't we talk tomorrow?" Jake pressed the door open and walked into the room. Melanie shook her head and closed the door behind him. "Look, I'm really too tired for this."

"You're part of our family now. Get better standards."

Melanie stared at him, her mouth hanging open. Finally, she collected herself enough to respond. "Excuse me?"

"You heard me," Jake sneered. "Don't sleep with the hired help."

Her hands flew to her hips as she took an angry step forward. "Who I sleep with is none of your damn business!"

"I thought you were different. You seemed to have a brain. Clearly I was wrong."

"Did you just call me stupid?"

Jake pretended to applaud her. "You were the one hooking up with Raymond at your father's wedding reception."

Melanie screamed in frustration, throwing her arms out to emphasize her anger. "We didn't hook up!"

Jake took two steps toward her until he was standing just inches from her, forcing her to look up at him. "I know what I saw," he hissed.

"You saw me biting Raymond's shoulder to get him off me." She met his cold stare with one of her own, her voice emotionless.

"Wait, what?" He took a step back, his anger replaced first with confusion, then disbelief.

He glanced down at her chest, then back up at her face. This time she saw something else in his eyes: lust.

Melanie glanced down to see that her robe had fallen open, revealing more cleavage than would ever be appropriate. She turned around as she hastily secured the robe once more, although she was really trying to hide her reaction to his obvious desire for her. "You heard me," she said over her shoulder, willing her heartbeat to slow to normal.

"Did he force himself on you?"

She chewed on her bottom lip until she tasted blood, then chided herself. Why was she so nervous? And why the sudden urge to explain herself to Jake, whom she'd likely see only two or three times a year at best—assuming she came back at all? Surely she could withstand his surly glances at her for those few days. In fact, maybe the timing had been perfect after all. He would think that she still had feelings for Raymond, whom he clearly despised, and would leave her alone. No more unsuspecting kisses or public displays that only served to embarrass her. Melanie told herself this was the best outcome in the long run. So why didn't she feel happier about it?

"Look, Raymond has his own demons to fight. They're none of your concern."

He grabbed her elbow and spun her around, pulling her so close that his lips were just inches from hers. "Did he?" He spoke through a clenched jaw, fighting to control his anger. The pure rage in his eyes scared her, especially as she was in a hotel room, naked under her robe, alone with this man.

"Let go of me." She sounded more confident than she felt.

The grip on her arms tightened. "Tell me!" he snarled.

Melanie straightened her spine and pulled back her shoulders, standing to her full height to look him squarely in the eye. "Let go or I'll scream." She spoke quietly, but she knew he didn't doubt her for an instant.

He stared at her, his eyes softening as well his grip. His jaw relaxed as his anger disappeared—no, not disappear, not exactly. More like he was tucking it back into place, hidden from the prying eyes of the world.

Realizing that he was fighting his own demons, Melanie's knees wobbled. She focused on staying upright as she fought an intense urge to pull him close to her and hold onto him, telling him that everything would be all right. She could see in the way he looked at her that he wanted the same thing.

She inhaled a shaky breath, overwhelmed by the power of her desire for the man standing so close to her that she could feel the warmth of his body, smell the hint of beer on his breath. She wanted him, more than she had ever wanted any man. The realization was both exhilarating and terrifying. The only thing she was absolutely certain of was that if she went to bed with Jake Monroe, she'd never find anyone else to measure up to the intensity she felt with him. Her body was screaming for her to rip off her robe and throw herself at him, but she couldn't move, afraid she might do just that. She looked into his eyes, willing him to understand, begging him to make the decision that she was afraid to.

When he left her standing there and walked out the door, Melanie finally exhaled. She collapsed on the bed, wanting to scream, but she wasn't sure if it was out of relief or frustration.

Chapter Twelve

Jake stormed down the hallway, barely controlling his emotions, thankful he didn't encounter any staff members as he slid out the back door and headed for his truck. The last thing he needed right now was for his staff to be terrified of his black rage. And they would be terrified, of that he had no doubt. What he wanted more than anything was to find Raymond and strangle him until the scrawny excuse for a human begged for mercy. Jake would wait until he felt the life leaving Raymond's body and only then would he drop him to the ground, letting him gasp for breath.

He slammed his truck door. Well, maybe he would let go. Maybe he wouldn't. No matter what happened, Raymond wouldn't be touching women other than his wife, and he certainly wouldn't be touching Melanie ever again. Jake cranked the ignition and growled. Melanie was his.

Just as quickly as his anger had surged upon hearing Melanie's explanation, it now drained from him, leaving him shaking in its wake. What did he mean, Melanie was his? He'd just met the woman, and yes he was attracted to her, but he barely knew her. He certainly had no claim over her. Melanie wasn't the kind of woman to be claimed. She was the one who did the claiming, although he wasn't sure she realized that herself. His lips curled into a smile. He saw it in her, in the way she stood her ground by the side of the road, on the stairs when she wasn't worried about how intoxicating her beauty was, in the hotel room when her robe slipped open, revealing soft mounds of flesh that even now made him wish he had pushed the robe open just a little farther, shown just a little more of the heaven that he knew it hid. Such a woman should never be restrained or claimed or possessed.

He leaned back against the seat, exhaling slowly, trying to block out the image of her staring him the eye, her chest heaving in anger, her robe falling open just enough to hint at the pure ecstasy it held. How was it that seeing her fully covered in a robe made her even sexier to him than when he'd seen her in her lacy bra and panties? It didn't make any sense. None of it made any sense. How had this woman invaded his life so deeply, so completely in just a few hours?

His heart thumped in his chest when he remembered what she'd said. She hadn't hooked up with Raymond. Jake had assumed he had interrupted them, yet she said she bit his shoulder to get him to stop. So she didn't want Raymond, despite certainly trying to protect him when Jake confronted her.

Not protect. Excuse his actions, even dismiss them, but not protect.

Jake turned off the ignition and rested his chin on the steering wheel, more confused than ever. He should never have gone to her room, should have just ignored the call from the receptionist and stayed in the bar, nursing his beer while monitoring Bruce Garrison. If only Bruce had acted up in some way, followed his usual course of action, Jake might have had an outlet for his frustration and then he could think more clearly.

The night was still young, though, and Bruce had a few more hours of drinking before the bar closed. Perhaps Jake still had a chance. He slid out of the truck and headed for the bar once again, refusing to think about the auburn-haired vixen under the same roof.

On any other night, Jake would have been thrilled with how calmly Bruce was drinking his beers.

Tonight, however, the calmer Bruce acted, the surlier Jake became. When the bartender told them it was last call, Jake almost goaded him into a fight. Luckily, Bruce stood up, threw a couple of bills on the bar, and walked out. Well, lucky for Bruce, but not so for Jake, who downed the rest of his beer and ordered a shot of vodka as a chaser. He didn't like to drink in front of his staff, but he needed to make sure he would be able to fall asleep without thinking about Melanie any more. Besides, nursing two beers all night couldn't really be considered drinking.

He dropped a twenty-dollar bill on the bar and headed for the room he used when he was in town. He didn't mind living in the hotel, especially as he was usually in town for only a week or so at a time. However, tonight he was really wishing he had a place somewhere in town, somewhere far from her. He slid the master key card into the lock but didn't open the door. His mind screamed at him to open it, to go inside the room and close the door behind him, locking himself away until the morning, when he could sort things through more clearly.

But he chose to listen to the other voice, the one that told him it would only be polite to check on her and make sure everything was okay. After all, he'd left in such a hurry. What if she panicked? Called Raymond to warn him? Called her father.

He smiled as he stepped to the door directly across the hall from his. She hadn't called her father because his mother would definitely have called and read him the riot act. His cell had been silent since the message that Melanie had checked in. And Raymond was too cocky by far. If she'd called him, he would've come down to the hotel for a showdown. Well, he wouldn't come himself; he would call the sheriff. But the sheriff was nowhere to be found, which meant that Melanie hadn't called anyone. She didn't care what happened to Raymond.

Or she cared enough about Jake to not want him to get into trouble.

That glimmer of hope was the only motivation he needed to slide his master key card into her lock.

Chapter Thirteen

The empty wine bottle sat on the table. The sweet drink had not calmed Melanie down, as she'd hoped, and now she paced in front of the bed, unsure of what to do. She did not call anyone. What would she say if she did? That Jake was angry and itching for a fight and Raymond was the likely recipient? Her father would just want to know why Jake was all riled up and how she knew. Those were subjects she thought best not to broach with her father. Plus Evelyn might not like being disturbed so late, especially tonight of all nights, only to find out that her son was being what she would most likely perceive as chivalrous. Calling Raymond to warn him offered no better options. If his wife answered the phone, how would Melanie explain Jake's anger without having to share details that no wife wants to hear, especially a very pregnant wife. No, it was better to let this play out however it was meant to happen.

Every time she heard a sound in the hallway, she raced to look through the peephole or press her ear to the door. When she heard a car in the parking lot or saw lights flash, she ran to the balcony door and pushed her face against the glass to look out. Soon all the sounds stopped, but there was still no Jake. Of course, he probably didn't even plan on coming back to see her tonight. Maybe she'd imagined his interest in her. Maybe he'd found someone else to satisfy his lust. Maybe he and Raymond were sitting at a table somewhere, having a good laugh about how they played her.

Melanie finally flopped down on the bed, her overwrought emotions exhausting her. Raymond had made his bed, so to speak. Yes, she'd come home to win him back, but she'd told no one of her plans, and all desire to be with him ceased the moment she met his wife. Melanie rolled over on her side. That wasn't exactly true. If she were honest with herself, her plan had been in serious jeopardy the moment she'd seen that cowboy get out of his truck to help her on the side of the road. Her brain just took a little longer than her body to catch up with reality.

Although she hoped the wine would silence the thoughts whirling in her head, it only made the thoughts take on a more provocative tone, punctuating her imagination with visions of Jake's kisses all over her body. Her body clearly knew what it wanted. Of course, her brain argued the point, but her body was winning by a landslide. No one could blame her for wanting to have a little fun, and a weekend fling would be just what the doctor ordered, wouldn't it? She had no doubt that Jake would be able to work out every kink in her body so she could wake up tomorrow refreshed and ready to take on the world. Her brain was still arguing though. If she acted on her feelings, it could make for awkward family get-togethers. And what if it turned out that they didn't get along at all, that it was just a physical attraction?

Melanie giggled. A physical encounter was all she wanted. She was still adamant about no long-distance relationships. Jake probably wasn't even relationship material. All she wanted was a one-night stand, no strings attached. If it was good, she might come back and visit more often. If it was bad, she could always get too busy at work to visit. She didn't want to fall into the Raymond trap again, where she was pining over someone only to have those feelings unrequited. Jake's casual flirtations from their first meeting and his good looks led her to believe that he liked having fun as well, so she didn't think he would pressure her for any kind of commitment. The fact that Jake was hell-bent on hurting Raymond proved to Melanie that he at least had some respect for women. It really was the best of both worlds for her: satisfaction with no commitment.

If only he would hurry up and come back to her. He would come back, right? Melanie let out a slow breath, telling herself to be patient.

Raymond didn't stand a chance. She willed Jake to go easy on Raymond. Yes, Raymond should get what he deserved, but Jake didn't need to get in trouble, and as much anger as had flashed in his eyes, she hoped he could control it. If not, he'd probably be calling from the jail. Or worse. What if he killed Raymond?

Melanie sat up, blinking as her eyes adjusted to the lights that she hadn't bothered to turn off. "He wouldn't, would he?"

"Wouldn't what, darlin'?" Jake was leaning heavily on the open door, a key card in his hand.

"How did you get a key?"

He wiped his hand slowly across his mouth. "Um, it's my...my...I know someone."

Melanie's eyes narrowed.

He wobbled as he stepped into the room to close the door behind him.

She laughed. "You're drunk."

"Am not. But I have had a drink. Or two."

"Just a drink or two?" She giggled, thinking about the wine. She didn't feel drunk, but she knew her inhibitions were impaired, to say the least.

"Would I have been able to make it back here if I were drunk?" He glanced around the room, smiling. His eyes came to rest on Melanie, and she saw him take a sharp breath in. "Sweet Jesus, you are beautiful."

Looking away demurely, she realized that her robe had fallen open, revealing her nakedness underneath. She pulled it tightly around her.

"No, please, don't do that." He stepped toward her, his eyes burning brightly as he licked his lips.

Melanie studied his shirt pulled tightly against his broad chest and tucked into dark jeans that made it all too easy for her to see that he was aroused. She let the robe relax slightly open, watching his reaction. His breathing became heavy, and he groaned lightly. She felt bolts of electricity shocking her skin everywhere his look traveled. She would go mad if he did not touch her soon. The robe fell back to reveal one breast. He licked his lips again. She wanted to feel his tongue caressing her entire body. She arched her back slightly. It was the only invitation he needed.

He stretched out on the bed next to her, kissing her deeply, their tongues chasing each other back and forth. She could taste just a hint of alcohol on him. When he struggled to remove his clothes while maintaining the connection with her, she reached out to help, only to fumble with the buttons on his shirt as well. He stood up to rip off his shirt without ever taking his eyes from hers. After he removed his pants, she let her gaze travel the length of him, appreciating each muscle of his body until she saw that he was fully ready.

"Melanie, you are sorely testing me," he growled as he returned to her side. He drew her breast into his mouth, his tongue circling the nipple until Melanie thought she was being consumed by fire from the inside out. She moaned loudly, thinking the whole town could hear her. She didn't care. Let the whole town know what they were doing as long as he didn't stop.

His mouth left her breast to travel up her throat to her ear. "I don't think I can wait."

She turned his face toward hers and kissed him, tearing down all her walls and giving herself to him completely. Finally she pulled away just long enough to whisper, "Then don't."

She spread her legs slightly, and Jake shifted to lower himself between them. She clung to his back, pulling him into her, feeling him fill her completely as she wrapped her legs around him.

His head lowered to kiss her, his mouth demanding and urgent. She arched up to meet him, matching his urgency.

"Mel...I can't—"

"Don't wait. Now...now!"

She shuddered her release. A second later, she felt him climax, then he collapsed on top of her, both of them panting heavily.

Melanie smiled. He was so much better than she anticipated.

Chapter Fourteen

Jake slid his hand down her stomach, letting his fingers trace across her skin, still amazed at how quickly he was ready for more. "So now are you glad you came back for the wedding?"

Melanie looked at him from the corner of her eye, one eyebrow arching.

"Your dad wasn't sure you would come back."

She rolled onto her side to face him. "It's not that I don't like coming home."

"You're a big city gal. I get it." He rested his hand on her hip.

Propping herself up on her elbow, she frowned. "No, that's not it."

"I meant no offense."

"Everyone always gives me grief about living in Chicago. I lived here for nearly twenty-five years, and I've been in Chicago for a couple of years now, yet somehow I am seen as a traitor to the rural life." She flopped onto her back, scowling at him when he chuckled. "Not like you'd understand anyway."

"Oh, you might be surprised." He leaned in and nuzzled her neck.

"Is it really so bad to want to experience new places?"

"You mean, like here?" He kissed her shoulder, then moved down to her belly button. "Or here?" He drew a lazy circle on the back of her knee with his fingers. When she tried to snuggle into him, he pushed her onto her back once again, laughing. "Not yet. I'm not done playing."

She closed her eyes and turned her face away from him, but he could still see her smile. He was moving his hand up her thigh and across her abdomen, his fingers so light against her skin they barely touched her. Her flesh broke out into goose bumps, as if anticipating his caresses. The reaction nearly drove him over the edge with desire, but he focused on her. He wanted her desire to match his own. His fingers continued moving up, going between her breasts, then circling one and then the other in wide circles. He circled her breasts again and again, each time moving almost imperceptibly closer to her nipples. Just as he was about to cross the tender flesh, he made the circles wide again.

"Not fair," she breathed, then bit her bottom lip. "You're torturing me."

"Now you know what you were doing to me all day today." He sucked her earlobe into his mouth and nibbled on it gently as his fingers continued their circles. She arched her back, moving one of her nipples into the path of his fingers, then moaned at the heat searing across her skin.

"Naughty girl." His hand moved back to her abdomen as a whimper escaped her lips.

When she looked at him, losing herself in his gaze and moving her hand to his stomach to trace his muscles as they tensed under her touch, he had to use every ounce of his determination to control himself. How was she doing this, arousing him so quickly, so deeply?

"Jake, please."

The words weren't much louder than a whisper, but they created in him a desire so intense that he hesitated, afraid that moving would cause him to lose all control. His breathing was ragged as she pulled him down on top of her so his mouth could trace the path that his fingers had been following. Melanie pulled his mouth to her breast, holding him there until he slid his hand between her legs. She opened herself to him. He touched her, tentatively at first, then she shifted her hips to give him full access. He moaned against her nipple.

He lifted himself to look down at her, his fingers still stroking her. "Say my name again."

She smiled a slow, sultry smile. "Jake. Jake, please, come to me."

The second time they orgasmed even more quickly than the first time—a feat neither of them thought possible.

Chapter Fifteen

Melanie stretched against the cool sheets, rolled onto her side, and blinked against the morning sun. She could hear birds chattering on the balcony, as if they were figuring out the day's plan. The chirping almost lulled her back to sleep once again, but the nagging voice in her head chastised her. It was morning and time to be responsible again. Last night had been…well, she couldn't pick just one word to describe it, but it made her practically giggle thinking about it again. Today was a day for clarification: This was a one-time event, and she was heading back to Chicago this evening. Surely Jake wouldn't put up any arguments, but it could easily become an uncomfortable subject. She kept her back to him while she rehearsed several possible ways to approach the topic. She closed her eyes. Every segue seemed so lame to her.

She wondered if they had time to play around a bit more before her lunch meeting. No, better to shut that thought down before it went too far. If they started something today, she'd never make it to lunch on time. She probably wouldn't get out of bed all day. Too bad. She wouldn't mind doing a bit more exploring. If only she had one more night in town.

Her eyes flew open. Why not? She could change her plane ticket to the first flight out tomorrow morning and still make it to the office by noon. Plus, if she were in a hurry to get on the road in the morning, there wouldn't be any long drawn-out anything. They could end it all quickly, with no one's feelings getting hurt. She smiled and rolled over to share her idea with Jake.

Except Jake wasn't in bed with her. A note on the pillow, written in a clear, confident hand, said, *Here's to experiencing new places.*

She chuckled at the reference, then rolled her eyes as she got out of bed. So much for worrying about how best to end it. She could take a lesson from him. He clearly knew how to extricate himself from potentially difficult situations without upsetting the other party, a skill likely gleaned from lots of practice.

After glancing at the bedside clock, Melanie rushed to take a shower. It was almost noon—how had she slept so late? She'd have to hurry now if she wanted to get ready and checked out before meeting her father and Evelyn for lunch. She didn't have time to consider the implications of Jake's note. Or the lump of disappointment hiding in the back of her throat.

Melanie walked into the hotel restaurant a few minutes after 1:00, wearing khaki shorts and a cotton top. Still feeling slightly flustered from her race to get ready, pack her bags, and check out, she stood in the entryway, looking for her father. The wedding gift that she'd forgotten to leave at the party was clutched in her hands.

The restaurant was small, with only about ten tables that she could see, but they were all covered in white tablecloths and the room was tastefully decorated in a neutral palate of earthy gray tones, creating an upscale ambiance despite the loud conversations coming from the patrons. Two waitresses dressed in white button-down shirts and black pants were moving throughout the room, refilling water glasses and speaking to their customers. The shorter of the two, a strawberry blond with pronounced dimples and expressive blue eyes, laughed a bit too loudly while talking to one of her customers. It was a laugh that was instantly recognizable as over-the-top flirting. Melanie shook her head. Some things never changed.

A chuckle in response made her heart skip a beat. The waitress moved on to another table, leaving Melanie with a direct view of Jake. What was he doing here? Her brain was screaming at her to hide, to leave before he saw her. Last night was done, it was over, she didn't need to see him again, not yet, not when a simple smile from him or a touch could create more cravings, more desires that had to be satisfied. But her body didn't listen, and she was still standing there watching him when he noticed her and stood to wave her over. Her feet moved of their own volition, carrying her to his table while she swallowed repeatedly, trying to overcome the dryness in her mouth.

"Morning." He leaned in to kiss her, but at the last moment turned his head so his lips barely brushed her cheek. Even that contact was almost more than she could handle.

She sat down before her knees gave out, setting the gift in the middle of the table. Melanie tried to think of something safe to talk about, something that wouldn't immediately bring up images of him touching her body and causing her to lose control in the most delightful ways, but her brain couldn't seem to get past the memory of his burning kisses or the feel of him inside her.

"Sorry we're late," her father said, startling Melanie from her thoughts as he pulled a chair out for Evelyn. "Told you the preacher was getting long-winded."

Melanie looked up, grateful for the distraction. "No worries." Her voice still somewhat shaky. "I just arrived myself."

Her father smiled and winked at her as he sat down.

"Oh, I am starving this morning," Evelyn said, then turned to Stan and giggled. "Gonna have to get my strength back up."

Stan patted Evelyn's hand. "For you my dear, anything you want."

Evelyn called over the flirtatious waitress, whose name tag said Trish, and asked about the day's specials. Jake's knee brushed against Melanie's under the table then jerked away quickly. The brief touch sent heat surging up her leg, and her body demanded more. She tried to focus on what the waitress was saying, knowing that if she looked directly at Jake, she might just maul him on the spot. Melanie stifled a giggle as she thought about just what would happen if she started ravaging Jake at the table in front of everyone. Her father was fairly open-minded, but even he had his limits.

Trish took their orders, ending with Jake. "And for you?"

Jake glanced up at Trish and winked. "The usual, darlin'."

Trish winked back. "Not a problem." She gathered the menus, flashed another smile at Jake, then headed off to the kitchen.

Melanie wanted to trip her and send her flying across the room.

"So what's this, sweetie?" Evelyn's question brought Melanie out of her visions of Trish landing face first in a well-placed bowl of potato salad.

Melanie moved the wrapped box closer to Evelyn. "Your wedding gift. I forgot to grab it out of the car yesterday."

Evelyn grabbed Melanie's hands in her own and leaned close. "Honey, just being here was gift enough."

Melanie blushed. "Thank you."

"And I will accept this gift on one condition," Evelyn continued. "That you come back to visit more than once a year."

"Here, here," Stan said, raising his glass of water to Melanie. He clinked glasses with Jake, who wouldn't look at Melanie.

"I promise to do my best," Melanie said.

Evelyn eyed her for a moment, then patted her hands. "That's all I ask. Now hand me that box." Her eyes lit up when she saw the crystal punchbowl, and she held it protectively while showing it to Stan.

Melanie's father rolled his eyes playfully. "Well, now you're gonna have to come back for many,

many visits, Mel, because this one is gonna want to throw a party every night!"

Trish returned with their salads, and Evelyn was quick to show the waitress the crystal bowl. To the girl's credit, she oohed and ahhed appropriately, which made Evelyn glow with pride. Trish set the last salad plate in front of Jake, then rested her hand on his shoulder. "Anything else?"

"We're good, thanks," Jake said.

Trish patted his shoulder, glanced around the table, then moved on to a neighboring table, where a tall man was calling "Miss, Miss" in an increasingly irritated tone.

Melanie stabbed at her lettuce with a fury that she told herself she had no right to be feeling. She was the one who wanted a fling, and Jake had given her exactly what she asked for. He'd even given her an easy out, practically handing it to her on a silver platter. But no matter how hard she tried to convince herself that everything was exactly as it should be, she couldn't get past the hurt she felt seeing him flaunt his conquests in front of her.

After they finished their lunch, Trish brought them coffee and cleared the remaining plates. Evelyn placed the punchbowl in the middle of the table, still obviously giddy over her gift.

Stan turned to Jake. "Missed you at the meeting this morning."

Jake smiled like a kid caught with his hand in the cookie jar. "Yeah, sorry about that. I just couldn't tear myself away from a previous engagement."

Meeting? Melanie cast a sidelong glance at Jake, who seemed intently focused on his coffee. Sundays were the one day her father relaxed, making exceptions for only two events: church and his AA meetings.

The blood drained from Melanie's face. Was Jake in AA? But he'd been drinking last night when he came to see her. A queasiness rose in her stomach no matter how strongly she concentrated on pushing it back down. If he'd been drinking, it was her fault. She could have spurned his advances from the beginning, but she didn't. She could have clarified the Raymond situation before it got out of hand or, better yet, let Jake think that she had been the initiator. Instead, she'd played right into his anger, letting her passion and desire for him trump all rationality. He'd gone out to right the wrong that Raymond had committed—something that Melanie had already done in her mind—and when he returned to her, she never even asked him what happened.

"Everything okay, Melanie?"

When she heard her name, everything seemed to crash down around her. Her breathing became shallow. She was desperately trying not to look at him. She knew if she did, if she looked into his eyes or saw him flash his smile, she was done for. She would give up everything—her job in Chicago, her life, her freedom—just to spend more time with him. Jake was the kind of man worth risking it all, and she had no doubts that it would be a tremendous risk. They might last a few months, maybe even a year, but men like Jake weren't satisfied with just one woman. Raymond certainly wasn't. And then where would she be? Stuck back in Bender with no career, no life, just another one of Jake's conquests. Not that Jake was even interested in her anymore. Was that why he'd left so early, why he was flaunting his closeness to Trish in front of her—because he held Melanie responsible for him falling off the wagon?

Just like Raymond had.

A coldness settled in over her heart. She would not risk that kind of humiliation, not again, no matter how loudly every fiber of her being was screaming at her to do just that.

She took a steadying breath. "Listen, I can't—we can't—do this, not here, not now."

She pushed back from the table. Both Jake and her father stood up as she did, and she could feel the concern as they reached out toward her, but she shook them off. "Fine, I'm fine. I just—I can't."

She heard a loud crash from the table next to them, followed by the irritated voice that had been calling Trish earlier. "What do you think you're doing?" It was a shriek that silenced everyone in the restaurant, and Melanie held her breath, afraid they would hear how close she was to hyperventilating. "Get your manager—I want you fired!"

She heard Trish's sob, then saw her streak past the table.

"Sir, let's speak outside." Jake's voice was calm, controlled, and Melanie's heart shattered. He was more concerned about helping Trish.

She turned to tell her father she was leaving, but she heard the unmistakable sound of a fist connecting with a face. Was this what he did to Raymond last night? Was this how he handles problems? Set to leave, Melanie gave Jake a final glance, but all she saw was his back. The angry customer, who was several inches taller than Jake, pulled back his fist and punched Jake in the stomach, hefting him into the air. Without thinking, Melanie reached out and snatched the crystal bowl off their table seconds before Jake landed on it. But her hands were shaking, and the bowl slipped from her fingers, crashing to the floor and shattering into tiny pieces.

"No!" she sobbed, looking down at the shards of glass all around her.

Chapter Sixteen

Jake heard Melanie's shriek, followed by her sobbing, and completely forgot about Bruce Garrison standing over him, waiting to finish what he'd started. The punch hadn't been much, certainly nothing Jake couldn't handle, but it had upset Melanie. Now he felt the overwhelming need to tell her he was okay while also wanting to jump up and shout from the rooftops that she cared about him. At least she didn't want him to get hurt.

But when he turned to look at her, she was staring at her own hands, tears rolling down her face. He saw the shattered glass all around her feet and his elation was replaced with fear. Fear laced with a blackness that made him want to throttle Bruce. Luckily for the other man, the hotel staff were on high alert. Two of the kitchen staff, two quite burly men who Jake had brought with him from the last hotel he opened, were already escorting Bruce from the restaurant. Bruce was yelling and fighting his escort, but one look from Jake and Bruce was practically pulling them to the exit.

Jake rolled off the table and swept Melanie up into his arms, holding her tightly against his chest. She continued sobbing, her entire body shuddering each time she inhaled for yet another sob. He waved off her father as he carried her to the front office area and placed her carefully into an office chair. Grabbing the first aid kit from the wall and slamming the office door, he told himself it was to protect her privacy, that it had nothing to do with the fact that his hands were shaking or that his panic was rising. She was still sobbing and didn't seem to be calming down. He squatted in front of her, carefully examining her legs.

"I don't see any cuts."

The tears fell faster.

"Are you hurt?" He held her hands and looked up into her face, but she turned away from him. "Mel, darlin', please. Tell me what's wrong." When she still wouldn't look at him, he pulled her up to sit in the chair, holding her on his lap. He rocked her lightly, terrified by the fact that he couldn't get her to stop crying.

After several moments, Jake considered calling 911. He was out of his depths, but he didn't want to let go of her for even the few seconds it would take to fish his phone out of his pocket.

Melanie took several deep breaths, forcing herself to calm down. "I'm fine." Her voice cracked, and she sat up, turning away from Jake to wipe the tears from her face.

"Melanie." He cleared his throat, further unnerved by how shaken his own voice sounded.

She pushed herself off his lap to stand up but still didn't look at him. "It just startled me, I guess."

"Are you sure?" He reached for her elbow, but she pulled away.

"Yes, everything's fine. Sorry about…all that." She half-turned and waved her hand, forcing a smile.

She wasn't fooling him and they both knew it. Jake waited, his breathing shallow. Whatever was happening, he had a bad feeling that he was not going to like it.

"Listen, I'm sorry, but I can't do this. Please, explain to my father." She didn't give him a chance to respond before throwing open the door and racing out through the lobby, to the large glass doors that led to the parking lot.

Jake watched her go, unable to breathe. The sucker punch she'd leveled at him hurt more than anything Bruce Garrison had ever thrown. Finally Jake gasped, as if his breathing returned all at once. He ran his hands through his hair and bent over his knees. He'd gotten exactly what he'd been looking for: a one-night stand who was gone the next day. No strings. No drama.

And she'd left him doubled over and gasping for breath.

His fury catapulted him into action, and he stepped through the glass entry doors just as her rental car pulled out onto the highway, heading south. Toward the airport, no doubt. Jake scowled. His anger settled around his shoulders. He tried to shrug it off, but he knew it would be a cold day in hell before he forgave Melanie Olson.

Or forgot her.

Chapter Seventeen

Melanie drove back to Chicago instead of flying. It would give her the time to work through the pain, get it all out of her system, before facing her colleagues at the publishing house. She avoided the interstate and the never-ending calls from her father, preferring to follow the two-lane highways so she could pull over whenever her emotions got the better of her. Which they often did. At some point in central Iowa she was able to admit to herself that she had feelings for Jake— she didn't understand how it had happened so quickly, but that was not the point. Admitting the problem was the first step. That night, after stopping at a small hotel in eastern Iowa, she emailed her father and told him not to worry about her, then climbed into bed and tried to let go of the memories of her night with Jake.

Thirty minutes later she knew sleep was not in the cards. She turned on the television, muting the sound, and watched the pictures flash across the screen, hoping she could trick her mind into thinking about anything but Jake and how she had run away from him. It was a cowardly thing to do, and when did she become a coward? She had never been afraid to speak her mind, which was one of the reasons she had landed her executive editor position, yet when it came to Jake...oh sure, she could tell him exactly what she thought about every topic in the world except one: her feelings for him.

She scoffed and swung her legs off the bed. "Don't be stupid, Mel."

Perhaps some work would help her get her mind off Jake's smile, his kisses, the way he made her toes curl when he touched her.

"Oh for crying out loud. Yes, he was good in bed—clearly from lots of practice!"

She snorted as she pulled out her laptop. Now she was openly talking to herself. Jake would certainly get a kick out of that. When she talked to him, she'd have to remember to tell him about it.

Except she wouldn't be talking to him. She wouldn't be going back to Bender, not while he was there. She could not—would not—be responsible for yet another man in her life turning to alcohol. Alcohol had destroyed her parents' marriage and it had turned Raymond into something he wasn't. Jake had been playful while drinking, but he'd also said he'd only had a drink or two. What would happen when he had more than a few drinks? And he inevitably would. They always did. No one ever fell off the wagon for just a drink or two.

He had a right to know why she walked out on him today, if only to avoid an awkward situation in the future in case she ever went home again. She couldn't imagine that now, but she knew that with time and distance she would forget how she felt now. The last thing she wanted was for Jake to expect her to jump into bed with him whenever she came for a visit.

She began to type the letter.

As the sun rose on the third morning, she saved the document and stood up to stretch. For the first time since checking into the hotel, she pulled back the curtains. The window looked out over a nearly empty parking lot. Melanie smiled. It could have looked out over a nuclear dump and she still would have smiled. Nothing could dampen her elation.

The letter had morphed into a retelling of her history with Raymond, an attempt to explain to Jake why they could never be together again. She stopped avoiding her pain and even wrote about her trip home, complete with all the daggers and bitterness. It was a painful process that led to more tears, but at one point she was able to remember past the pain and write about unknowingly being attracted to her soon-to-be family member, highlighting the humor in the situation. Now, more than seventy thousand words later, along with a whole lot of caffeine and very little sleep, she had written a novel. "My novel," she whispered. She clasped her hands and bit the knuckle of her forefinger to keep from screaming with excitement.

It was a rough draft and undoubtedly needed a lot of work, if she ever even tried to publish it, but it was done. Somehow she didn't think she'd ever show this novel to anyone. It was too personal, too heartbreaking. Yet she had written her first novel, and if she could write one, she could certainly write more. The exhilaration that coursed through her was almost as intense as what she felt when she was with—

"No, I won't think about that. Not yet."

She shook her head as if to prove it to herself, then checked her cell phone for messages. The phone was dead, and it took her a moment to remember where the charger was. When she finally plugged it in, she groaned. Seventeen voicemails.

Several messages were from her dad, with him doing his whole nonchalant check-in that he had mastered long ago. He gave her a random update, like how Evelyn had moved his shampoo to make room for all her toiletries, then ended the message with some version of "hope everything is good with you." It was his way of saying that he was worried about her and that she needed to call him.

A couple of messages were from work. They were worried about her. She hadn't bothered to inform them of her change of plans. If she didn't show up by 8 a.m., she would be out of a job. She glanced at the clock on the nightstand. It was just after 6 o'clock and Chicago was another three to four hours away. Her dream had always been to be a writer; she couldn't put that off any longer.

She wouldn't put it off any longer. She was no longer an editor. She was a writer.

Two of the messages were silent. She sat on the corner of the bed and listened, imagining that she could hear his breathing, feel his heartbeat. But then he hung up, and the connection was gone. Gone without saying a word.

Just as she had done to him.

She slept for nearly two full days before finally checking out of the hotel and driving back to her tiny apartment in Chicago. During the drive, she decided what she would do. She had enough money saved up that she could live for several months—maybe even eight or nine if she were careful about expenditures. She would devote herself to writing full time for at least three months, then maybe find a part-time job if she wasn't feeling confident. Three months. She could do that, right?

It turned out she could quite easily. She put her first novel aside and delved into a story about three elderly sisters, including all the imagined husbands they'd married and buried. That story turned into several more, and soon she had the outline of their antics as they traveled the world, carrying out special jobs that involved the removal of unfaithful lovers and husbands, somehow always managing to clear the way for true love. The irony that she was writing a romantic comedy was not lost on Melanie.

Energized by her writing and its new direction, she rarely left her computer. She tried to follow a more or less normal sleeping schedule, but she often woke in the middle of the night with an idea that she convinced herself she had to write up at that very moment. Eating occurred only when her stomach's growling got too loud, and more often than not she ordered delivery food rather than taking the time to cook. Her only focus was on getting the draft of the romantic comedy done. An insistent power was driving her to finish, get the ideas out of her head before they disappeared forever.

With only two chapters left to write, an idea for a third novel burst into her thoughts. She scribbled down notes, then ordered Chinese delivery, racing to see how much of the final two chapters she could write before the food arrived. Just as she typed the first paragraph of the last chapter, the doorbell rang. She jumped up and did a little dance through her living room. She was nearly done, and that familiar ecstatic feeling was begging to be released. She threw open her door, singing, "Hello, Mr. Chinese delivery man!"

Except it wasn't the Chinese food at the door.

"Hey, darlin'."

Chapter Eighteen

Melanie felt all her energy dissipate. "What are you doing here?"

He smiled, waiting. He nodded toward her apartment.

"Please, come in." She said it with as much boredom as she could muster.

He meandered silently about the living room while Melanie watched him. He glanced at the coffee table full of pizza boxes and empty cans of soda, then looked up at her, his eyebrows rising in a question.

"What are you doing here?" she repeated.

"It's been radio silence for more than a month."

She crossed her arms tightly over her chest and frowned.

"Look," he said, running his hands through his hair. "I don't want to be here any more than you want me here, but your dad asked me to check in on you." He huffed loudly. "And then when I stalled, my mom told me to get over here pronto. She's a nice woman, but you don't say no to her."

Melanie remained silent, watching him from hooded eyes. He took a few steps toward her desk, glancing at the papers spread out on it.

"New book?"

She ignored his question. "So you expect me to believe that you came all the way from Nebraska just to check up on me?"

Jake looked at her and blinked. "No."

"Right, so why don't you tell me why you're really here."

"No," he said slowly. "I don't expect you to believe that I came all the way from Nebraska because I didn't."

Melanie waited for him to explain.

Jake shuffled his feet, glancing up at her. "Melanie, I live in Chicago."

She stared at him for a moment, not moving. Finally, she said, "Bullshit."

"Now why would I lie about something like that?"

Melanie shook her head. "You were driving a Nebraska truck. I saw the license plates."

"Ah, you caught me." He smiled and shrugged. "Small towns are more amenable to listening to my proposals if I arrive in a local truck." When she didn't respond, he continued. "Technically, the truck is registered in my mom's name."

She loosened her arms a bit. "What do you do?"

"Property manager." He glanced down at her desk again, picking up a sheet of typed paper. "We build hotels, get them established, then turn them over to local management."

He seemed distracted as he spoke, and Melanie realized that he was reading the page. She snatched it from him.

"Hotels? Wait—you built that new hotel in Bender?"

He frowned. "Yeah. Managed it for a while too. How else could I have gotten a key to your room?"

"You remember that?" she asked, her voice barely audible.

His frown deepened, his eyebrows furrowing together. "I'll never forget that night. Trust me—I've tried."

And there it was. He wanted to forget it, forget her. She bit down on her bottom lip, trying to stop the tears that she knew were coming. "You need to leave." She turned her back to him. When he didn't respond, she reached out to the door and opened it. "Please. I can't be responsible for you falling off the wagon again."

"What the hell are you talking about now?"

She jumped at how close he was behind her.

"You know what I mean. Just go."

He walked around to stand in front of her, pushing the door closed. "Melanie, I did not fall off the wagon." He enunciated each word.

Why was he doing this to her? "You said you had been drinking that night."

"Yeah, I had a couple of beers in the hotel bar. I was trying to figure out whether I should kill Raymond or not for what he did to you."

"Right, a couple of beers."

"So?"

"So! And then you missed your morning meeting with my father."

Jake's eyes darted back and forth for a moment, then he looked at her and burst out laughing. "Melanie, I'm not in AA."

She shook her head, confused.

"That was a meeting with the locals about turning over management of the hotel. I was only in town for the weekend, so we scheduled it for Sunday morning before church."

Now it was her turn to frown. "But you missed it."

"Yeah, because I didn't want to leave you."

"But you did." This time she stepped away from him, putting more distance between them.

He murmured something under his breath and rolled his eyes. "Only because Trish's idiot boyfriend was there. I didn't want to wake you up, so I went to the lobby to call and postpone the meeting, except when I got there, one of our waitresses, Trish, and her boyfriend—you may remember him, he's the one who cold-cocked me twice at lunch—were having a heck of an argument. I asked him to calm down, and he said he would, but I didn't believe him."

"For good reason, it seems."

"Right? So I went back to the room to leave you a note, then went and sat in the restaurant at the table next to his so I could monitor the situation." He rolled his eyes. "Worst three hours of my life, especially since all I wanted to do was be with you."

Melanie's heart fluttered at those words, but she forced herself to remain calm. "Wait a minute. You're not sleeping with your waitress?"

He crossed his arms. "I don't sleep with the help. Not like—"

"Not like me," she finished for him, wincing.

Jake ran his hand through his hair. "Okay, look, I checked on you like they asked me to. Call your dad. Let him know you're still alive."

He was halfway out the door when she stopped him.

"You didn't beat Raymond up?"

He turned back to sneer at her, then adopted a more neutral expression as he spoke tightly. "No, your precious Raymond is unharmed."

Melanie swallowed past the lump in her throat and took a step closer. "And you didn't fall off the wagon because of me?"

Jake shook his head.

"And you didn't want to abandon me that morning?"

Jake stared at Melanie for several beats. "Is that what you thought of me?" He laughed until he was nearly doubled over. "Sweet Jesus, no wonder you ran away so quickly."

His laughter was infectious, and soon Melanie was giggling at the absurdity of it all. She really had messed up everything, just not in the way she thought she had.

As her laughter died down, she said, "And you live in Chicago."

"Yes, darlin', I do." He stopped laughing and looked at her with pure desire—a look she matched. "So did I really make you woozy?"

Melanie blinked several times, trying to grasp what he was talking about.

He held up the typed page he still carried, reading from it. "Seeing him step out of the truck, I finally understood what it meant to feel woozy—and it was a feeling I never wanted to forget." He looked up at her and smiled. "Woozy, eh?"

"Oh, yes," she said softly. "Very, very woozy."

Jake stepped toward the door, clearing his throat uncomfortably. "How much do you have left on your novel?"

"What?" Melanie's body was screaming about being denied the pleasure that was within reach.

He pointed at the desk. "Looking at that stack of papers, it looks like you're almost done."

"One chapter left." Her brain struggled to shift gears. "Tying everything together."

He looked at her, and her breath caught in her throat when she saw the passion burning in his eyes. A familiar warmth traveled the length of her body.

"You've got one hour. Get everything done by then."

Melanie tilted her head to one side, her confusion obvious. Jake grabbed her in his arms and kissed her so deeply that her knees went weak and she sank into him. In that moment, all the desire she'd tried to ignore for the last several weeks came roaring back to life and it was ravenous. She wanted him—she'd always wanted him, and she'd do anything to have him, over and over again.

Just as quickly he pulled back and whispered to her in a husky voice. "When I get back, you're all mine, Melanie Olson."

He turned and walked out of the apartment, leaving Melanie clutching at the sofa for support.

Chapter Nineteen

Melanie held her first book release party the following spring in a small independent bookstore in a suburb of Chicago. Mostly older women attended the event, which started with Melanie reading a section from her novel. Afterward, she signed copies for her guests, thrilled by the steady stream of fans that left her hand tired and cramping.

"Nice work, Mrs. Published Author," Jake said, sneaking a quick kiss on her cheek before sitting down next to her.

An older woman wearing a large pink hat stood next in line for an autograph. Jake winked at her, and she giggled coyly. "My, you're quite the rapscallion, aren't you?"

"Yes, ma'am, I am." He leaned across the table. "I'm the inspiration for all the rapscallions in the book."

"Oh I'm sure you are, sir." She giggled again and handed her book to Melanie. "Now this is for my sister, Clara. She will think your story's a hoot!"

"Thank you," Melanie said.

"Just you wait until the next book comes out." Jake pretended to be sharing an insider secret with her.

"Oh, I hope it's soon."

"It's already printing as we speak." Jake stood and walked around the table. He towered over the woman but bent down to continue their intrigue. "I tell you what. You give me your address, and I'll make sure you get one of the first copies of the second book—before it even hits the stores."

The woman's eyes grew large with excitement, and she looked at Melanie for confirmation.

"He's a man of his word, ma'am." She handed the signed book back the woman, then smiled at Jake as he escorted her to the counter, where he took down her address while she told him how jealous Clara would be when she heard about this. Melanie shook her head, laughing at her husband, the flirt.

The bell at the door to the store jingled and Raymond walked in. Jake was still deep in conversation with the older woman, who was talking about her sister.

"Hey, Mel. See you finally published something."

"Yes, I did. Did you want me to sign your copy?"

"Oh, you know." He stuffed his hands into his pockets. "I left my copy at home. I'm living here now, in Chicago."

Melanie forced a smile. "Really?"

"Yeah, a couple of months now. Anna left me."

He paused to glance at Jake. Melanie remained silent.

"So, uh, maybe I can stop by and see you sometime, get my book signed."

"Sure, sure, let me just check with Jake about when our schedule is free. Jake?"

"Oh, you know? Why don't I just buy another copy while I'm here, save us all the trouble?"

Melanie shrugged. "Your choice."

Raymond headed to the checkout, nodding to Jake as he passed. When he returned, Melanie wrote "Thank you" in the book and signed her name. They shared a few more polite words, then Raymond left.

"Should I be jealous?" Jake said as he watched Raymond leave the store.

Melanie stood and planted a kiss on his lips. "Absolutely not." She smiled. "In fact, you should thank him."

"Thank him?" Jake nearly choked on the words.

"Of course. If not for him, I wouldn't have returned for the wedding, and then I wouldn't be all yours." She raised one eyebrow and smiled at him in a way that she knew he couldn't refuse.

He grabbed her hand and pressed it to his chest. "Darlin', you drive me crazy." He leaned forward to kiss her. "And I love you for it."

He jumped up to run out of the store after Raymond, but paused at the door, then sauntered back to Melanie. "I'll thank him later. For now, I want to hear more about how you're all mine."

Acknowledgments

Deciding to write a book is easy. Seeing it through to the very end is the real challenge. I have been lucky to have the support of so many people during this endeavor.

I must thank my fabulous writing group. Although spread out across the country, we hold each other accountable every single day (Jules Dixon!), pushing ourselves to write ever better. I love that we demand the best while remaining supportive and encouraging. I also want to thank Lisa Kovanda, Victorine E. Lieske, and G. M. Barlean for being such exceptional role models in independent publishing.

I am eternally grateful to my beta readers, who dissected each draft of this story while asking for more. There is nothing more encouraging for an author than when the fans ask for the next book.

Finally, my deepest thanks go to my brother, Brandon, who has continued to support me in all my writing efforts in unexpected and inspiring ways.

Turn the page for a sneak peek at

A Heart's Promise

Book 2 in the Great Plains Romance series

Trish reached up and pulled her strawberry-blond hair over her shoulder to braid it, her fingers quickly working through the long tresses. It was a habit she'd picked up since her parents' death. Sitting in the hospital after the accident, waiting for news about her parents, she'd braided and unbraided her hair hundreds of times. Now it helped her think, her brain working through the problem as her fingers worked through her hair.

She didn't want to leave Bender, but with no job and no place to stay, she didn't think she had much of a choice. If only she had found work on a farm, she wouldn't be having this problem now. Unfortunately not many farmers were willing to hire female managers, not even the corporations that were snatching up the farms at an alarming rate. Trish had spent the small savings her parents had left her for her degree in agri-business—a sound investment everyone had said at the time considering her goal of managing and eventually owning her own ranch—but now here she was, about to lose her waitressing job. The few hundred dollars left in her bank account would not sustain her through the end of the month. Her fingers reached the end of the braid, paused, then pulled it all out. She combed through her hair and started braiding once again.

"Excuse me."

The deep voice startled her, and Trish focused on the tall man standing a few feet in front of her. How had someone so tall, so imposing, sneaked up on her without her noticing? She suppressed a shudder and dropped her hands to her lap, affecting the polite pose her mother had taught her was appropriate for ladies. "Yes?"

"I'm looking for Jake Monroe."

"Just through there. Follow the hallway until the end. The front desk will know where he's at."

"Thanks." The man reached for the door, then glanced back at her. "You okay, miss?"

"Oh, no need to be dusting off your white hat." She shooed him toward the door.

"Well, you certainly don't look like a damsel in distress, it's just..."

Trish watched him, curious about what he would say.

He shoved his hands in the pockets of his faded jeans and pursed his lips. "It's just, you look like you need a friend right about now."

She crossed her arms in mock indignity. "I'm pretty sure eavesdropping on ladies' thoughts will get you kicked out of the White Hat Club."

He shrugged. "Their meetings are pretty boring."

"I know, right? It's all 'I saved this damsel, I saved that kitten'—we've heard it all before. Where's the excitement?"

"In the Black Hat Club, naturally."

Trish raised an eyebrow. "Oh, you're one of those."

"Gotta be true to who I am." He reached out a hand. "Dalton, by the way."

"Nice to meet you, Dalton By The Way. I'm Trish On The Bench."

His handshake was firm but relaxed. Still, Trish could feel an intense power pulsing just beneath the surface.

"So, Trish On The Bench, can you help a fellow out?" Dalton sat down next to her. "I'm kinda overdue for my White Hat badge this month."

"Fine." She rolled her eyes in an exaggerated fashion. "But don't say I didn't warn you. This is pretty boring stuff."

Dalton cleared his throat and turned to focus all his attention on her. He reminded her of a little boy trying to prove what a grown-up he was. Trish couldn't help but smile.

"Oh a smile! One point for me."

Trish applauded. "Nicely done. Now try this one on for size: My jerk of a boyfriend—make that ex-boyfriend—just punched out my boss, so I am pretty sure I'm gonna lose my job."

Dalton laughed a deep, throaty laugh that Trish felt rumble through her core.

She rolled her eyes. "Great. At least I can still entertain a handsome stranger."

He placed his large tanned hand over hers on the bench. "Jake's not going to fire you for what your ex does."

"It's not the first time he's caused trouble." Trish pulled her hand out from under his, pretending to check her fingernails as she wiped away invisible dirt. In reality she'd been disturbed by the surprising heat his hand had generated in her, sending shocking warmth reeling up her arm.

"So why have you stayed with him?" His caramel-brown eyes studied her face.

She shrugged. "Nobody else needs me, I guess."

He frowned.

"Plus, he owns my apartment complex." She nudged his shoulder with hers. "Not smart to piss off both the landlord and the boss in one day, but that's how I roll."

Trish glanced up when the service door opened. Jake stepped outside and looked around until he spotted them on the bench. "Hey, Dalton. Sorry man. It's been a crazy day."

"Yeah, I was just hearing about it." He didn't take his eyes from Trish.

Jake clapped him on the shoulder, then motioned for Dalton to follow him inside. "Oh, hey Trish, go talk to Mrs. Jackson in the front office."

Trish gave Dalton a "told you" look as Jake led him inside. Only after he disappeared through the door did she realize she'd been holding her breath.

Books in the Great Plains Romance Series

Vibrant Heart

When the ever-organized Melanie Olson returns to her small Nebraska hometown to prove to the commitment-phobe Raymond what a mistake he made, a flat tire threatens to ruin all her plans. Luckily, cowboy-turned-entrepreneur Jake Monroe stops to help the woman stranded by the side of the road, unaware that his world is about to be turned on end. Realizing that she's traveling to the same wedding he is, he decides fate has dealt him a winning hand—until he discovers that she only has eyes for the town womanizer. Jake is determined to get the beautiful spitfire to look his way, but her intensity might be too much for even him to handle.

A Heart's Promise

Trish Cassidy is an easygoing woman with a goal: to manage her own ranch. But after her parents' death, she finds herself stuck with a dominating boyfriend who has probably just ruined her last chance to connect with the local ranchers. Just when she thinks she must give up on her dream, the enigmatic Dalton James steps into her life, offering an opportunity to build a ranch from the ground up. What she doesn't expect is her powerful attraction to her new boss—or how controlling he starts to become.

When Dalton James decided to build his horse ranch, the last thing he anticipated was saving a damsel in distress. Then again, Trish Cassidy isn't someone who needs saving. So why is he so protective of her? More importantly, why does he feel like he has to do the right thing around her, even when she doesn't want him to?

Heart So Sweet

With four older brothers, rancher Susannah Clark is used to dealing with men and getting them out of trouble. But when her childhood crush Tate Trudell returns as sheriff of Harrington County, Susannah must decide whether to save her brothers yet again, even if means losing the man she loves.

Tate Trudell never expected to move back to Harrington, especially after how he left things with his best friend, Lucas Clark, just before Lucas left for the war in Afghanistan. But a lot has changed in ten years, including Susannah, Lucas' little sister. When Tate discovers that her passion matches his own, he's determined to be with her. To get the woman of his dreams, he must work through his bad blood with the Clark family—if Lucas doesn't kill him first.

So Wills the Heart

When the tough gets going, artist Evie Jacobson runs away. So when her great aunt leaves her a property in rural Nebraska, Evie uses the opportunity to escape her boss, who's deluded himself into thinking she loves him. But life in the country is a bit too tame for Evie—until she meets Jonathan Clark, a man who tests the limits of her spontaneity. When Evie discovers that Jonathan might not be everything she expected, will she runaway yet again or will she have the strength to stay and face her greatest test?

Jonathan Clark's afternoon break from working the ranch turns into a fantasy-come-to-life when he encounters Evie Jacobson skinny dipping in a private pond. His water nymph's playful side excites him like no woman he's ever met, and he looks for any excuse to be with her. But a rancher's work is never done, and Jonathan must choose between his family and Evie—a woman who might have already moved on to someone else.

My Heart, My Gift

Can the big city girl convince the small-town cowboy to give Christmas a second chance? Or will the secret she hides destroy any chance of a relationship between them?

When Serafina Anderson makes a mess of her first semester of college, she does what she knows best: avoids facing her parents. This time she runs away to spend her winter vacation at the ranch of her cousin, Trish. Her escapades also lead her right into the arms of Andrew Clark, the small town's most notorious troublemaker. But Sera sees beyond Andrew's crass nature and recognizes that the bad boy isn't as bad as everyone makes him out to be.

Andrew Clark hates Christmas—at least he has since his parents died. He refuses to buy into the commercialism of the holiday and does his best to shove the hurt he feels down so deep inside him that no one will ever find it. So when Sera ignores his bad temper and rude remarks, he wonders if he's finally found the angel who can rescue him from himself—until he discovers that she's been lying to him all along.

About the Author

Corrissa James was not always a country girl. In fact, she fought it all her life, traveling the world to live in far-flung cities like St. Petersburg, Russia, Caracas, Venezuela, Varanasi, India, and Guadalajara, Mexico. She didn't realize she was meant to live in the country until she returned to her roots in Nebraska, where she discovered the beauty of the fields around her (even if she was allergic to them) and the intensity of Mother Nature (who sure packs a wallop!).

Corrissa wrote her first romance stories in junior high, although at the time she didn't really know what happened after kissing, so she improvised with lots of ellipses (…). Her professional writing career initially took her away from romance—but never far away as Corrissa could always be found with a romance book at hand.

Today she focuses on western romance novellas, offering afternoon reads focused on strong women and the men they choose (never without some struggles along the way).

If you've enjoyed this book, please leave a review.

Thank you!

Check out more works by Corrissa James and see
what's coming next by visiting
www.corrissajames.com

www.ingramcontent.com/pod-product-compliance
Lightning Source LLC
Chambersburg PA
CBHW051247170626
46809CB00004B/1538